A VILLA IN SICILY:

FIGS AND A CADAVER

(A Cats and Dogs Cozy Mystery—Book Two)

FIONA GRACE

Fiona Grace

Fiona Grace is author of the LACEY DOYLE COZY MYSTERY series, comprising nine books (and counting); of the TUSCAN VINEYARD COZY MYSTERY series, comprising six books (and counting); of the DUBIOUS WITCH COZY MYSTERY series, comprising three books (and counting); of the BEACHFRONT BAKERY COZY MYSTERY series, comprising six books (and counting); and of the CATS AND DOGS COZY MYSTERY series, comprising six books.

Fiona would love to hear from you, so please visit www.fionagraceauthor.com to receive free ebooks, hear the latest news, and stay in touch.

ISBN: 978-1-0943-7350-8

CHAPTER ONE

Every time Audrey went for a walk in Mussomeli, she was reminded of how much she loved this town, smack in the middle of the island of Sicily.

The town, with its old, quaint homes, nestled together atop a hill, was full of baroque architecture, the smells of fresh-baked Italian treats mingling with cool sea breezes and fresh mountain air, and locals and other one-euro home buyers, all waving hello to one another. The sun was usually bright and the weather, a temperate seventy degrees. Though a lot of the homes were rundown, their foundations nearly crumbling to ruin, the place exuded all kinds of possibilities, and a promise that one day, she'd be living in the Mediterranean home of her dreams.

At first, Mason, her handsome American contractor friend, with his long, athletic strides, was two steps ahead of Audrey, but as they got closer to the place on the map that Orlando Falco, president of the town council, had provided, Audrey picked up the pace, breathing heavily. By the time they made it to *Via Barcellona*, the street where the property for the new veterinary center was located, she was practically running.

Mason broke into a jog and easily caught up with her. "If I didn't know better, I'd think you wanted to get rid of me."

Not much of an exerciser, she could barely get the breath into her lungs to talk. When she did, it came out in huffs. "I'm just... really excited... can't wait... to get this place set up... and start getting real clients."

"Yeah. Let's not put the cart before the horse. I hope it's not in too bad shape."

"No. The councilman told me it only needed minor cosmetic touches. I bet we can have it up and running in a week."

Falco had stopped by the day before and given her directions to the property, in the form of a hastily hand-drawn map, and the key to the front door. The deal was that the town would provide the property in exchange for her services, and provide a generous allowance to get the place fixed up and in working condition. Audrey peered down at the map and up at the numbers, trying to find the right building among a patchwork of closely packed, nondescript storefronts. She looked up and squinted.

"Should be around here somewhere."

They went past an old Catholic church with a statue of Mary in front, and a town square with a little fountain. Falco had said it was very centrally located, off the square, prime real estate, which had made Audrey wonder, for a blink, why another shop owner hadn't snapped it up sooner. But she'd been too excited to question Orlando Falco, who was her friend. She stopped, spinning in place, trying to orient herself.

"Is that it?"

Mason pointed across the street to a small storefront with a sign in front that said, *Affittasi Commerciale.*

She turned the paper around and checked the number on the door, 135. "Yes, that could be it! I think it is!"

She practically skipped over to it and stood in front of it, taking it in. It was a narrow building with a paper-covered window, so she couldn't see inside, but it was constructed of red brick and had a pretty turquoise-blue door with a glass doorknob and little brass mail slot. She'd only ever worked for a large veterinary practice, in Boston. Never had she had her very own place. She shivered with excitement, imagining the words *Mussomeli Veterinaria, Dott. Audrey Smart* painted across the window in regal script.

And yes, it was almost directly across from the town's square, a stone's throw from the pretty fountain. She turned back to it, her heart thumping like mad.

"Oooh! It is prime location! It looks nice! Don't you think it looks nice?" she asked Mason, jostling his arm a little. She couldn't seem to speak in any voice other than childishly excited.

He had his hands in his pockets and was eyeing the place a bit more skeptically. "Why don't you save your excitement until we get inside, Boston?"

"Yeah, well, I can't wait," she said, rushing across the sidewalk to the front door. She stuck the old key in the lock, twisted it, and pushed open the door… to the most horrific stench that had ever invaded her nostrils. It hit her like a wall, making her step back onto Mason's toes.

"Ow, hey—" He paused for only a beat. "What died in here?"

Audrey winced. She wasn't sure she wanted to find out, but then again, she'd gone through hell and back with her little place. She'd seen some pretty gross things, from green, furry mold to a sink so clogged with someone's long black hair that she retched the entire time she was cleaning it out. Nothing could scare her now.

Holding her nose, she pressed forward. There was a little reception desk in the front, then off to the right, natural light poured in through the huge, arched storefront window, lighting up an absolutely gigantic room. "What do you think this was before?" she asked, stooping down to pick up something among the discarded junk. "Oh. That's what this was!"

It was an advertisement for a vacuum. She showed it to Mason, whose eyes bugged out like he'd never seen one before in his life. He'd pulled the top of his Pink Floyd T-shirt up to cover his nose, baring some of those abs. Brina would've approved... and wanted her to snap a picture.

"An old vacuum store," she explained, trying to ignore them.

"Vacuum store?" Now he was thoroughly confused. With his drawl and the resultant nasal twang from holding his nose, he sounded a little like a sad country song. "You mean, this place just sold vacuums? Why?"

Sometimes he could be so clueless. It was almost as if he'd lived in another world, before this. She ignored him and went to the storefront. "This is where the waiting area can be," she said, imagining it all perfectly in her head. She climbed over a broken display rack, still full of brochures for some extremely ancient vacuum models, and waved her hands. "If we put a wall up here, separating it from the back, we'll probably need two or three exam rooms, a kennel, a supply closet... you think chain-link kennels would be best or should we try to go greener and more animal friendly?"

Mason's eyebrows tented. "Uh, Audrey..."

"Probably greener. I bet people around here appreciate green businesses. Maybe it'll have tax benefits. Oh, look!" She raced to the back of the place. There was already a hallway in the back of the store, covered in old, wooden paneling, heading toward two rooms. She threw open the doors. A tiny little lunchroom with an old vending machine and a small bistro table, and a tiny bathroom with peeling bubblegum-pink tile. Perfect.

"You know, girl," he called to her as she rummaged around in her purse for a pen or pencil. She needed to start writing down a list of supplies. "I may be a damn good carpenter, but there's no way on God's green Earth I'm going to have this place ready for you in a week. I hope you realize that."

She smiled as she finally located a Bic pen in the deep chasm that was her hobo bag. "You can do anything you put your mind to," she said, mimicking something her father used to tell her all the time when she was young. "I have faith in you."

His eyes ping-ponged around the vast space. "That makes one of us."

Audrey studied him, dread pooling in her stomach. The last thing she needed was him giving her a dose of reality. If she couldn't open the place soon and start getting some paying customers in, she'd be sunk.

She forced the thought away. "Oh, come on. It's perfect. Look." Turning the map over, she started to sketch out her idea atop a glass display case. He peered over her shoulder, laughing a little, but it wasn't his usual laugh. She paused and looked at him. "What?"

"You have mighty high aspirations for this place. How much are they giving you to fix it up?"

"Two thousand euros," she announced proudly.

"Yeah, um. Aud? Hate to break it to you, but just one of those walls you're talking about is going to blow your budget out of the water. And that's materials alone. You're not even talking about labor."

Right. Labor. *His* fee. That was really all he cared about, since he definitely wasn't here for the animals he despised so much.

"Well, they want me here so badly, maybe they can give us more, if I ask. I mean, I'm the one single-handedly solving their stray problem. They should be willing to cough up big bucks for that, right?"

"Here? In Mussomeli? Good luck with that," he muttered as he kicked through a pile of assorted garbage—old food containers, cardboard, dust bunnies, and broken pieces of furniture. "These people aren't exactly rolling in bucks, in case you didn't notice. I mean, vacuum guy didn't make it. What makes you think you will?"

"I will, because I don't suck." She grinned.

He crossed his tanned arms. "Don't try to be funny. It doesn't work for you."

"Then don't be a downer," she said, heading toward one wall. "Right over here is where the cats can be. We're going to need at least twenty spots. Maybe more. There are a lot of strays out there and I'm going to want to have a place where they can get out and explore."

"Um, Audrey ..."

He was just going to throw his rainclouds everywhere.

"We can't very well have cats and dogs in the same spot. So, more walls. One right here, and—"

"Audrey ..."

"Maybe we can have the surgery over there. A prep room, too, obviously. My office should be pretty big, well, not crazy big, but big enough for three people to meet, because I'll need somewhere to consult with patients' owners about treat—"

He dropped the T-shirt from his face. "Audrey!"

She stopped. "What?"

He motioned with his eyes, down to her feet. There, right at her toes, was a mangled mass of fur. From the tail, it looked like a possum. Dead, and swarming with flies and maggots.

She shrieked and ran to Mason, nearly jumping into his arms. "Oh my gosh!"

He disentangled himself from her and peered closer at it. "That explains the stench," he said. "Let's see if I can find something to dispose of it."

They found a couple sticks, and, fighting the overwhelming need to vomit, Audrey and Mason finally scooped the thing into a plastic bag. She'd dealt with all kinds of horrible animal injuries before, but nothing was quite as disgusting as week-dead vermin.

"Poor thing," she murmured sadly as Mason tied the top of the plastic bag shut, leaving an oily stain on the floorboards. "I guess the first order of business should be getting some cleaning materials and throwing out the trash."

He nodded. "I know a guy we can get a dumpster from. Full-size. I think we're going to need it."

She rubbed her hands together. "Great! So when can we get started?"

Mason held up a hand. "Chill, girl. I'm starving. Why don't we get lunch and you can tell me what you need to have done?"

"I'm not hungry! And there's so much to do right now, I'd rather get going on this." She spun around in a circle. She wasn't sure what to do first. "And I'm paying you to help, not to go to lunch."

He rubbed his eyes tiredly. "Uh, Audrey ..." This time she looked at him, because the last time he'd used that voice, she was dangerously close to stepping in mutilated possum. "You know I'll do my best, but I do have my own renovation to deal with."

"I know, but—"

"I got to get it done by next month. I have someone from America staying over. To visit."

She frowned. *Someone.* Family? A friend? A girlfriend? That was kind of vague. Was he being so intentionally? "You do?"

He nodded and didn't offer more. She had to admit, it made her curious. If it was a girlfriend, that was kind of gross, the way he'd been borderline flirting with her. Actually, he really hadn't been. Most of his "flirts" were really just risqué jokes, like the offer to come upstairs and help her change. Audrey got the feeling he simply did it not because he was interested in her, but because he enjoyed seeing her blush.

Anything that might have been going on was really only in Audrey's head, and Mason was clearly a woman magnet, so his guest very well could be a girl. And that was *fine*. Perfectly wonderful. The poor girl probably needed all the prayers Audrey could throw at her, for having to put up with Mason. Then why did those first tendrils of envy creep in? "Um... who?"

"Someone. Not important. So yeah, like I said," he continued like he really wanted the subject dropped, kicking a wall with the toe of his boot. "I'm going to try to get over here and help when I'm not working on my reno, but I can't do it all."

"Oh, don't worry about that," she said, waving him off. "I expect to do a lot of it myself."

"You? With your own renovation?"

"Yep," she said, giving him a confident smile. "I've got it all under control."

He raised a doubtful eyebrow.

"What? I did masterful shower work."

"Yeah. I also think you called that shower every curse word in the book. And this is a little more than a shower, girl."

Okay, that was true. They'd discussed this before, and sure, it did feel like she had her work cut out for her. But she didn't have to make the place perfect. All she really needed were the kennels and a clean exam table to operate from. She'd make do. Besides, she didn't have any of her own family or friends—and definitely no boyfriend—visiting that would necessitate her speeding up her own house renovations. She had plenty of time to worry about the house later.

Just then, Orlando Falco walked in, a bright politician's smile on his face. The man was perpetually wearing a black suit and tie, even despite the warm temperatures.

"Good morning, good morning," he said, gliding over to her in his shiny Italian loafers and handing her a newspaper. "So you've found the place, eh? Pretty nice, don't you think? Great location."

She nodded. "Yeah... but now that I look at it, I think there are some things we didn't discuss. I think I might need ..."

She stopped when she noticed his face falling as he looked around the place. "You have not done much, have you?"

"Well, no. I mean, you just sent me the keys yesterday, so …"

She looked down and realized he was pointing to the rolled-up newspaper he'd just handed her. He grabbed it from her hands and opened it up, pointing to a large, half-page ad, with a bunch of Italian flags, confetti, and a picture of a cute little puppy. She smiled at it. "Nice. What does it say?"

"It's um… for the grand opening of this establishment," he explained.

"Oh. Advertising already?" she murmured, thinking, *Well, that's kind of premature, but whatever.* Then her eyes fell on something in the ad.

It said, *18 Settembre.*

September? Meaning, like, actually September?

She fumbled for her pocket, finding her phone, and looked at the calendar. "Wait. Are you saying you want this place open in… five days? And like, accepting patients and everything?"

Falco nodded. "I don't just *want* it, Audrey. It *has* to happen."

This had to be a joke. "Why *has to*?"

"Well, it turns out, the cats in this town are becoming a real menace. One of the council members seems to think we'd be better off euthanizing all the strays, and is pushing the council that way. I don't know how long I can hold them off from seeing her point of view."

"But …" She looked at Mason, who simply whistled.

Audrey's jaw dropped to the floor. *Okay, so forget about having everything under control.*

CHAPTER TWO

Caught under the sink in the prep room, trying to install a simple shelving unit, Audrey tossed back her head and screamed, as loud as she could, up to the ceiling.

The ding of her phone had distracted her, and she'd dropped the shelf before she'd pulled her hand away. Right on her pointer finger.

She pulled her swollen finger out from between the plank of wood and the brace, where it had unwittingly gone when she'd tried to fit it in there. She stared at it. It was bright red and starting to get purplish under the fingernail. It pulsed with pain.

"What made me think I had this all under control?" she muttered to herself, wondering miserably if she was going to lose her nail.

It'd been three days since she'd first laid eyes on this place and made that statement. Since then, it'd been like a tennis match, constantly springing back and forth between her house and the vet center. She hadn't slept more than four hours a night, usually falling into bed well after midnight, after putting out one fire or another.

She slid out from under the sink and rinsed the finger in cold water under the tap. As she did, she checked her phone. A text from Brina. *More pictures of abs PLEASE.*

Audrey sighed. Brina was a little obsessed. This morning, Audrey had sent her the one pic he'd taken a few days ago, and since then, Brina had been texting her non-stop, begging to make him a member of the family.

True to his word, "Abs" hadn't been around much at all. He'd helped with a lot of the major framing that needed to be done, but she'd seriously had to tone down her wish list to fit both her budget and time frame. She couldn't be angry at him, though. He'd done a lot of work, bought some lumber on his own dime, and hadn't asked for payment.

But the place was nothing like she'd hoped she could create when she first walked in. Instead of the center with her name on the front and different rooms for all the animals, all she had was a back room, a waiting room, and a kennel area. And none of them was furnished. Falco had stopped by a few days ago, saying he knew of an office up the street that was closing, and maybe he could get the furniture at a reduced price, but he hadn't been back since then.

It was okay. The animals weren't picky. She kept telling herself she'd be okay. She didn't have to have everything right away. Not that that helped much.

She got the feeling when Falco arrived that he'd expected her to have snapped her magic fingers and made the place a vet center. What did he think she was, Mary Poppins? All week long, it'd been pressure, pressure, pressure, to be ready for opening day. Now, though, she was more Zen about it. It was a work in progress. Everything would be okay.

Well, she *had* been more Zen about it, until she'd gone and squeezed her finger under a shelf.

She wrapped her finger in a paper towel and sighed as she slumped into a chair. It looked like another thumb, and the pain throbbed all the way up to her elbow. All the while, she kept spotting things that needed to be completed before opening day. Great. Now how was she going to finish things up?

She typed in: *You'll just have to wait,* with her good hand.

But that picture? :O. My ovaries! How can you stand to be around him without wanting to jump that?

Jump that? It must've been happy hour and Brina'd had too much wine. She forced away the temptation to do such a thing and continued to make that mental list of uncompleted chores, still thinking of what he'd said about the "guest" he had coming. Quickly, she typed in: *I think he has a girlfriend.*

A second later, Brina replied: *So what? Can't be serious if he didn't bring her with him.*

As she was about to reply with, *I think she's visiting him next month,* she heard the front door squeak open. "Hello?"

From the drawl, she knew it was Mason. "Back here," she called.

Just her luck. She was always trying to prove how capable she was to him, and yet every time she saw him, it was right after making some major mistake. There was no way to hide her extra thumb.

He appeared, looking that same combination of scruffy and scrumptious. Truly, that photo hadn't done him justice. The jerk.

"What happened there?" he asked immediately, zeroing in on her injury. "And why is your face all red?"

"Shelf one, Audrey zero," she grumbled.

"Girl. You need to chill."

"No time." She showed him the finger. "You think I'll lose the nail?"

He inspected it and shrugged. "You'll have time when you drop dead from a heart attack. Which judging from the way you're looking, ain't long."

True. How many times had he told her to calm down, because she'd been running around like a top wound too tight? The last few days, he'd stopped in during his lunch break for a few minutes, just to see how things were going before heading back to his place. Each day, she'd gotten more and more frantic.

"Okay, I'll try." She took a deep breath, let it out. "Better?"

This time, Audrey was surprised to see he had his toolbox with him. "Just sit there for a minute and catch your breath. I'd hate to have to haul your backside to the hospital," he said, looking around. "What do you need help with? The shelf?"

She stared at him for a moment, shocked. No way was she going to refuse the offer for help, since she'd come up with a list of about twenty things that Mason could probably do in three minutes that would take her the better part of an hour. That shelf being one of them. "I was just trying to finish with the shelving in the console under the sink."

He grabbed his drill and got to work immediately, setting it right. As she'd anticipated, it took him less than ten minutes.

As he wiggled underneath the counter, sure enough, his T-shirt rode up, exposing those legendary abs and the waistband of his boxers. He had an outie. Interesting. She found the heat returning to her cheeks, because it was simply impossible to look away. For a second, she wondered if it'd be too risky to snap a photo to satisfy Brina.

She finally managed to avert her eyes and said, "To what do I owe the pleasure? I thought you had a lot of work to do."

At that, he let out a groan. "I do. But I ran into a little roadblock. I'm waiting on a freaking inspection, and who knows how long that'll take."

She blinked in surprise. She thought she'd cornered the market on roadblocks, that for everyone else's renovations, it was smooth sailing. "Why?"

He exhaled. "Some woman came by my house yesterday and asked to see the renovations. I showed her all of it, including the new Jacuzzi tub and radiant heating I put in."

"Jacuzzi tub? Where did you get the money for that?"

"Never said I was poor, Boston."

She frowned. Gorgeous, handy, and rich? Wow, this guy definitely swam in the deep end of the gene pool. "You mean, you've got money? Like, what are you, a trust fund baby?"

He chuckled. "Something like that."

Wow. She imagined him standing out in front of his mega-mansion, sipping a mint julep, like one of those old southern plantation owners. "What are you doing here, when you have all that at home?"

"It ain't what you have. It's what you do with it that counts."

She stared at him. What a wise Buddha saying. She leaned forward, a little dazed, the pain in her finger forgotten. Then she realized she was in danger of drooling and straightened. "Oh, so. Yeah. What happened with this woman? She came to visit you? Who was she?"

He worked the drill for a second and then pushed out from under the sink, showing even more of his hard chest before his shirt fell into place. "Yeah, I thought that was her way of coming on to me. Little bit of a cougar, fine, but I don't discriminate. After I give her the tour, she goes and tells me she's a member of the council and I'm in violation of a bunch of laws I'd never heard of. So now I have to get an inspection to find out what needs to be fixed. It's a whole load of bull."

Audrey's eyes widened. "You mean you might have to take the tub and the radiant heating out?"

He nodded. "Might. Don't know. If so, I'll be out thousands. Thanks to Mimi Catalano, town councilwoman from hell. Word of advice—if a witchy woman with dark hair and red lipstick ever comes your way looking for a tour? Pretend you ain't home."

"I can't believe she did that!" Audrey exclaimed, indignant. "That's really snaky of her, to come in all sweet and after you do her a favor, giving her a tour, she drops that bomb on you? I mean, what gives her the right?"

"Besides being town councilwoman?"

Audrey frowned. Maybe she could talk to Orlando Falco about it. He was president of the council and he did like her. She wondered if she could soften the blow. "But really! Why? This town was dying, which was why they had the one-dollar house offer to begin with. They're begging for people to come in and remodel their houses so that they can breathe new life into the town. You'd think they'd go easy on us."

"Apparently not." He placed his drill back into his toolbox and looked around. "The good news—for you, anyway—is that I can help out around here as much as you need me. Can't do a thing in my house until this is resolved."

Audrey smiled. It was a little like winning the handyman lottery. "That *is* good news. But …" Her face fell. "What about your… guest?"

He shook his head, clearly pained. "They're gonna be SOL, I guess."

"So, who's coming? A girlfriend?" she asked nonchalantly.

That amused smirk appeared on his face. "What are you, jealous, Boston? I know. I'm like marmalade. It's a shame there ain't more of me to spread around." He winked at her. "So what do you got? Anything?"

Noting with some annoyance that he *still* hadn't answered her question, she filed through her mental list of tasks that had to be completed prior to opening, trying to decide on the most Mason-worthy; that is, so complicated she wasn't sure she could succeed on her own. She said, "I have a few new lighting fixtures that need to go in?"

"Lead the way."

She started to, but hesitated. "I should probably tell you now… I spent all two thousand euros on stuff for the renovation. You were right. It didn't go very far. And Falco said they didn't have anything left in the budget to give me more just yet."

He simply winked. "I figured. You'll just have to pay me some *other* way."

Where usually she blushed, this time, she simply said, "Ha ha, in your dreams," and led him to the boxes of light fixtures without much thought. Was it possible his effect was wearing off on her? She hadn't really giggled maniacally around him—her normal reaction around good-looking men—in a long time.

As he got to work, Audrey went to the front of the building to do some work, painting the walls of the waiting area. She'd chosen a pretty pale yellow, the same sunny color she hoped to paint the living room in her house when the time came. She'd just begun to pour out the paint when the door opened and G, her handsome Sicilian chef friend, walked in. "*Ciao,* I thought I could find you here."

He was definitely bigger in stature and rougher around the edges compared to Mason, with tattoos up his arms and a short buzz cut, but he had a boyish smile that made Audrey's stomach flip-flop, not to mention how nice he sounded whenever he spoke Italian to her. Plus, his *ciambotta* was to die for.

He had yet another bowl in front of him. She could smell it from here, and her mouth watered. "I brought lunch for you, *principessa.*"

Did he just call her princess?

Now she found herself giggling maniacally. She eyed the bowl. "Is that what I think it is?"

"Actually, it is a new spin on an old recipe. I just invent today. I thought I would let you try it, first one, *si*?"

She nodded eagerly, enchanted by the scent, her stomach rumbling on cue. "Yes, please." He set it down on the reception counter and pulled off the wax paper lid to reveal several small balls with a deep-fried crust. "What is it?"

"*Arancini di riso.* A specialty of the island, but I made it different. I add a little of this, a little of that. You try. You like."

She reached in and took one between her fingers. It was still warm. When she bit into it, a long string of cheese trailed behind. She'd had many a mozzarella stick before, and loved them, but whatever this was blew them out of the water. A light sauce dribbled on her tongue as the flavors melded in her mouth—the fontina cheese, pine nuts, and rice, along with the crispy crust. She let out a sigh of pure delight.

"Oh oh oh these are so good," she said, wondering if it'd be impolite to inhale the rest of them. She wanted to. Badly.

"What happened to your finger, *cara*?" G said, his voice turning concerned.

She looked at it. It was now a dark, angry purple. Blood was pooling under the fingernail. She wondered again if she'd lose it. "Oh. Little mishap with a shelf."

He suddenly grabbed her hand and held it up for his inspection. "Aw." He made a tutting noise, like she was a child. Then he kissed her knuckle, very gently, just brushing his lips over it, his goatee tickling her skin. Goosebumps popped from her arms. "Can I help you?"

"Hey."

She and G whirled in unison toward Mason. Somehow, Audrey couldn't get it out of her head that whenever the two men got together, they were sizing each other up, like competitors. For her. Which was obviously ridiculous, considering Audrey had trouble getting *any* guy to notice her, much less two gorgeous ones. Still, an icy chill settled in.

Audrey dropped her hand and did her best to chip away at it. "Hey, Mason. G just brought some of these incredible cheesy rice balls. You have to try one."

G didn't seem as eager to offer them to Mason, but he still held the dish out. "*Si.* Have one."

"Cheesy rice balls?" Mason lifted a corner of his mouth in disgust, as if she'd just said *fried monkey brains*. "Nah. I'm good."

Audrey would've argued, but she really wanted the rest of them to herself. She took another in her hand and prepared to bite into it, as the two men stared silently at one another. "Oh, uh, G. Mason already fixed the shelf for me, so I'm good. Now he's looking at some lighting."

"That is very handy of you," G remarked, reaching for her hand again.

Audrey snatched it away and said, "Um, Mason, did you finish already?"

"No. I had to ask you. That lighting fixture in the exam room, which switch do you want it to hook up to?"

"Oh. I'll be right there to check it out." Mason shrugged sullenly and went into the back as she looked at G. "Mason's helping me get things together. We're opening in a couple days. I can't believe it."

G looked around. "Ah. A couple days? You'll be ready for that?"

She followed his eyes and winced. The place was a wreck. The drywall hadn't been painted, the flooring hadn't been installed, not to mention that the exam room and surgeries were completely empty, save for the shelving unit Mason had just installed. She nodded. "Sure. Of course. At least, I hope. It's cutting it close, but the town council really needs the help. So if it's not all perfect, it's fine. It'll get there."

"You're a busy lady, Dottore Smart." He smiled at her, and once again, she blushed. "I've been trying to get you to go out on the town with me for ages, and you're too busy for me. When will you be free? You must have pity on me soon."

She laughed at his expressive way of talking. He spoke loudly and with great gusto, and he gesticulated wildly with those arms of his. He may have looked tough, but he was a teddy bear. And Brina was right—she should've been able to go on a date with him. A real date. He was a catch, after all. Not only was he handsome and funny and sweet, he could cook.

But now was not the time.

"I'd love to," she said, finishing off the last of the rice balls. "But I really can't yet."

He frowned, but his eyes twinkled. "You're not—how you say—playing games with me?"

"No." The thought that she could do that was hilarious. When it came to men, she never played. She always wound up the *playee*. "I'm so busy. Maybe when I have this place up and running, I'll have the time. Rain check?"

He gripped his heart dramatically. "You kill me, *principessa*. But yes, promise me?"

"I promise. Thank you for lunch."

He leaned over and gave her a very hearty kiss on both cheeks. Then he took his empty bowl and waltzed out the door. For a large man, he was surprisingly graceful on his feet. She peered out the door, watching him go, embracing or waving hellos to everyone he passed. He had such a crowd of admirers, and no wonder. He spread sunshine wherever he went.

She hardly noticed Mason behind her until he said, "You're really going to go out with that guy? Looks like a loser."

The tone of his voice was one of disapproval.

"I don't know," she said dreamily, as Mason's words fully registered in her head. She whirled to face him. If G was the ray of sunshine, Mason was the storm cloud. "No, he's not. He owns his own restaurant."

Mason snorted.

"It's better than being some entitled trust fund kid," she said. "Besides, why is it any of your business?"

He shrugged, ambivalent. "It's not. But you should. If that's what you're into."

"Maybe I will," she said, craning her neck to look out the door, but by then, G had already gone. "When I can find the time."

She scanned the mess around her, which looked nothing like a vet center at all, and sighed.

Which is probably... oh, just about... never.

CHAPTER THREE

As Audrey finished hanging the temporary sign on the front door—*Mussomeli Veterinaria, Dott. Audrey Smart, Opening Soon!*—she smiled. She'd constantly debated whether Sicily was a smart move, and she'd thought a million times about moving back to Boston. But this? This was a major step toward putting down permanent roots and making Mussomeli her actual residence. Soon, she'd have a permanent sign up, and she'd feel more like a long-term fixture in this town.

She was nervous, but it felt like the right step.

"It's crooked," Mason said to her, chewing on an apple, then tossing the core in the dumpster on the curb.

She scowled at him. "Thanks, Mr. Ray of Sunshine."

"What do you need, boss?"

"Just a few more things. I made a list inside. There's some heavy furniture I need help moving, and a couple of storage cabinets that should be nailed down, but I think we're almost done. I'm ready to greet my first customers."

She followed him inside to the reception desk. He set his toolbox down on it and looked around. "I gotta say, I did *good*. Never thought this place would shape up like it did."

"Yeah. Next time, you should charge for your services."

"You're funny."

It was rather nice. Once they got the sunny terra-cotta-colored paint on the walls and the laminate wood flooring in, it'd come along, and looked homey and welcoming. The furniture was almost in place, and the reception area was clean and white, with modern fixtures, almost like what she'd dreamed of. Sure, it needed some finishing touches, but she planned to add those later.

Audrey smiled proudly, too happy to even bother reminding him that *she'd* done a lot of it. Besides, he'd done her a solid, offering a lot of free labor. He deserved to have that ego of his stroked a little. "I couldn't have done it without you."

"True. You're lucky that witch of councilwoman spoiled my plans and put me at your complete disposal."

"Oh, right. Any word on that?"

He exhaled. "Not yet. I tried to call her office in city hall to smooth things over, give her a little bit of the Mason charm, but she hung up on me. Can you believe that? The witch." Clearly, he couldn't believe it, probably because he was so used to women hanging on his every word, so she shook her head. "Anyway, I'm still in a holding pattern. So when does the staff come in for training?"

Her smile faded. "Staff?"

"You do have staff, right? Like a receptionist? I mean, because you don't even speak the language, so I'd have to imagine it'd be pretty dang hard for you to …"

Her mouth fell.

"So that's a no, then?" He winced for her.

God. She needed one of those. Big time. Maybe she didn't need vet techs right away, but she'd at least need a right hand to translate. If only she could learn a little more Italian. Maybe then she wouldn't feel so lost. She'd gotten the hang of a few phrases, but it'd be better if she had someone in the practice who spoke …

"Um …" She wanted to kick herself. Of course, a vet didn't work alone. "Well, I—"

"You seriously didn't hire anyone to help you?"

She slumped over the receptionist desk. "No! God, how could I forget them? They were the glue holding the whole practice together, where I used to work! I'm toast!" She moaned, straightening immediately. "Wait. Maybe Falco has?"

Mason snorted. "Falco, the guy who gave you the key to this place and then ran off, never to be seen again? That guy's about as useless as the T in *pinot grigio.*"

He was kind of right. Other than checking in every once in a while and telling them where they could get various items they needed, he hadn't really been a man of action. That meant, likely not. Could she deal with all of Mussomeli's strays by herself?

No. No, of course not.

But she knew someone who could help her.

She grabbed her purse from behind the reception desk. "Can you do this list alone?"

He glanced at it. "Yeah. But… what are you gettin' in that crazy head of yours, girl?"

"Tell you later. I'll be back in a little bit. I have an idea."

She rushed outside before he had a chance to protest and hurried to G's place. It was just before the lunch rush when she went inside his little café and slipped onto a stool at the bar. He was busy preparing a dish and didn't see her until he delivered a pasta dish to another customer. "Hey! *Principessa!*"

"Hi!" She waved, smiling. His easygoing humor would be just the thing to calm her nerves.

She was about to order her favorite, the *ciambotta*, because there was no better comfort food than that vegetable stew and a hunk of crusty bread. But he held up a finger, then put a pasta dish in front of her. *"Pasta e fagioli."*

She inhaled deeply. "How do you say wizard in Italian? Because that's what you are!"

He laughed and pointed to the other customer, a man with a goatee and a NY Jets ball cap. Another American expat, drawn to Sicily by the one-dollar home deal. "Meet Bruno. He's from New York. You two are neighbors, yes?"

Audrey waved at the guy, who was built strong and refrigerator-like, like a football lineman. She had a hard time imagining someone his size fitting in some of the homes around here, since most of them had low doorways and smaller rooms, made for when people were a lot less substantial in stature. "Hi. I'm Audrey. From Boston. Where did you buy?" she asked.

"No, I haven't bought just yet. I'm here on vacation. Just testing the waters, so to speak," he said. "But if I like it, my girlfriend and I are going to move here and start over. We're both self-employed, so we can really work anywhere."

"That's great. That would be ideal. I'm a vet, so I'm setting up a practice in the area. It's a lot of work in addition to the house renovation."

"I bet." He'd been shoving an entire meatball into his mouth, and said what sounded like, "What's your house like?" but she couldn't be entirely sure because it came out as more of a grunt and a raised eyebrow.

"I moved into the house on *Piazza Tre* about a month ago. You're smart. I bought my place sight unseen."

The man raised an eyebrow. "No kidding?"

"Nope." She was proud of the fact, now, even though when she'd first taken it on, it'd felt a little like certain death. Whenever she began sharing war stories with the other ex-pats, it made hers a lot more interesting by comparison.

It got the desired effect. Bruno eyed her with admiration. "Wow. And you moved out here all by yourself? That takes guts."

Audrey laughed. "Or insanity. Or a little of both."

"And? How was it?"

"Oh, it's been a rollercoaster. But I guess that's kind of what you expect when you do something like this. I love it here, though. It took some getting used to, since I don't speak the language, but it's definitely growing on me."

He seemed excited to hear that. "This is all my girl's idea, really. She's been out here, visiting family in Palermo before. That's where she got the idea. My girlfriend speaks Italian fluently. I'm a different story, but I took a few classes at a community college before we started getting serious about this, so I know a few helpful phrases."

"That's great. That'll be so helpful. You'll probably love it."

"Yeah, well, if we're going to move out here, we want to get married before we do. So we're on a two-year plan. I still have to propose. She's got a lot of family. A lot of family. And if you ever hear of a New York wedding, you know they don't come cheap."

She smiled. "Yeah. Weddings rarely do!"

He checked his watch and threw a few euros down at his place setting as he struggled to pull his body out from under the counter. "Nice talking to you, Audrey, but I've got to meet with my Realtor. He's going to show me a couple properties on the south side. Wish me luck."

"Good luck, Bruno. Nice meeting you. Hope you propose to that girlfriend of yours and join us in the insanity, too!" She waved at him, watched him leave, and then hunched over her plate, practically inhaling her pasta. It was delicious, just the right amount of heat and flavoring, like almost everything G made her. Any girl who dated G would probably end up the size of a whale.

"So what is the latest?" G asked, leaning toward her on the counter. "The vet place open for business yet?"

"Almost. Couple days. Just waiting on the last permit."

"Ah. I am going to be your best advertiser. I'm going to tell everyone I know to bring their pets to the best vet in the area."

"The *only* vet, you mean. And I will tell all my patients' owners about your café. Do you have pets?"

He laughed. "No, just goldfish. Ha ha. That's all."

"Oh. You're so nice. I'm a little nervous, and that's why I stopped by. I'm hoping you can help me."

"Anything for you," he said in his deep voice that made her heart melt.

"I just realized I'm probably going to have to hire help. A receptionist or something. I need someone who speaks Italian. Are you going to come to my Grand Opening?"

He patted his chest. "Me? Wouldn't miss it."

She sighed with relief. One friendly face would be nice. And maybe he could help serve as translator. "Thank you." She yawned.

"You look tired," he observed.

"Yep. No sleep will do that to a person. I need a vacation and I'm not even in business yet."

He laughed. "I go away tomorrow. To Catania, for the day. A delivery I make. Would you like to come with me?"

"Catania? That's in the east, right? Mount Etna, the volcano?"

He nodded. "We see the sights. I show you. *Si?*"

The idea itself was an amazing one. Like a dream. Since arriving in Mussomeli, she hadn't left the town proper at all. Part of her dream of being in Sicily was exploring this beautiful land, and yet she hadn't done much of that at all. Most of the exploring she'd done had been while renovating the two properties.

"Well, I don't think so. I still have a ton to do, but ..." She thought of what Brina would say. Brina would've shoved her into his arms with both hands. Not that it was a date or anything. G was just being friendly to her. "I need to find a receptionist. If you know of anyone ..."

"No. I will be your receptionist, if you need me! You know me, I know everyone in town. I'd love it. Temporary. Until you find someone else, of course."

"Really? Well..." Out of excuses, she shrugged. "All right. Sounds great. Can't wait."

"Good. I come at nine and pick you up."

She smiled, doing her best to push all thoughts of the business away. Mussomeli had survived all these years without a veterinarian. It could survive one day more.

CHAPTER FOUR

Audrey rolled over in bed when she heard a knocking on the door.

She covered her head with a pillow and tried to drown out the sound.

When it clearly wouldn't go away, she sat up and looked at her phone.

It was precisely nine o'clock.

She jumped out of bed and peered through a crack in the shutters at the small white car pulled up in front of her house.

Outside, G was knocking, a single red rose in his hand.

So this *was* a date? Brina would be thrilled.

She sighed in awe, then realized she was in no condition to go on any date, with her hair a rat's nest and drool all over her face. Luckily, she'd spent last night trying to figure out what to wear. She'd been wavering between a sundress—romantic, in case it was a date, and a denim skirt and low boots—in case it was more of a friendly sightseeing thing where she'd need to be more active. She still wasn't quite sure, and she wasn't really sure what she wanted it to be either. Both outfits were hanging from the door, waiting for her to make the final decision.

She grabbed a robe, and pulling it tightly around her body, she opened the door, gnawing on her lip. "Uh, hi, G. You're early!"

His eyes danced with amusement over her state of undress. "I said nine, no?"

"Well, everyone's always so late in Italy, I just assumed you would—"

He shrugged. "No matter. You finish. I wait."

"Are you sure? I'm not going to make you late for your delivery?"

"No, no. I'm happy to make him wait for such a beautiful reason." His eyes drifted over her. He smiled, not in a creepy way, but it made her whole body blush, nonetheless, something likely very evident from her lack of attire.

She let him in and brought him up a couple of stairs, to the big living area she liked to call the ballroom. Even though it wasn't all that huge, it was certainly bigger than most of the rooms in these smaller homes. "Thank you. I'll only be a minute."

He looked silly, a big, tattooed man, falling into the dainty and feminine damask chaise in the room. "Take your time. This is a nice room, *cara.*"

"Thanks. Haven't fixed that one up yet, though." As she rushed upstairs and got herself ready, she told him a little about the supposed history of the place, and how a Sicilian noblewoman had used the place for her illicit affairs with a baron many centuries ago.

She threw on the sundress and sandals, shook out her hair, applied lip gloss, and met him downstairs. He eyed her with appreciation. "Gorgeous, *Principessa.* You look wonderful."

He was the perfect gentleman, leading her out to his car, settling her in the passenger seat before going on ahead to his own side. They chatted and flirted the whole way there, and as she expected, despite the cultural differences, he put her right at ease. He explained different points of interest and the history behind certain places, adding his own flair: "This is the village where my mother grew up," and "My father and I used to fly kites in this field." It made the two-hour drive seem like mere minutes.

As usual, he was very charming. But she wasn't sure if his interest was a romantic one, or if he was simply being friendly. The culture gap was one Audrey couldn't seem to grasp. He was so nice and touchy-feely with just about everyone. Maybe this was nothing special.

Before long, the sprawling, snow-capped peak of Mt. Etna loomed in the distance, its top disappearing beneath some hazy gray clouds. "Wow," she said, enjoying the view while taking in deep breaths of fresh, cool air from the open window. It was invigorating, inspiring.

This was exactly what she'd come to Sicily for.

Yes, she knew that she'd have to deal with setbacks and difficulties with the renovations, but she also knew those were temporary, and the reward afterward would be lasting. This felt like a taste of that reward. She'd told herself that if only she could be done with all the work… then she could finally *live*.

But there was nothing wrong with living right now. She needed to remind herself of that.

And having G as a boyfriend… that wouldn't be terrible. In fact, having a Sicilian boyfriend would probably make her transformation to a real Sicilian woman complete.

"What are you thinking, *cara?*" he said, snaking his hand over the gearshift and taking hold of hers. He squeezed it gently.

She smiled. "Just that this is great. Everything is so beautiful. And I think it might just make me never want to go back."

They parked at a side street in the center of the city, which G explained was the second largest in Sicily, and climbed the hilly cobbled street toward the bustling center of town. The sea air was cool, but not chilly, and smelled fresh and clean. Audrey smiled as they walked past a gelato shop with a cute little polka-dotted awning.

They stopped at an outdoor café for lunch, deciding to sit at a bistro table under a black-and-white-striped umbrella.

As they sat down, G pulling out the chair for her, making it scrape along the cobblestone street, she said, "What about your delivery?"

He gave her a sheepish look. "Ah, I make that part up. I make this trip for you. To get you out to enjoy the sun. Pretty thing like you should not be hiding away."

"Really?" She giggled. She spread the napkin out on her lap and looked around at the gorgeous architecture. The air smelled like the sea, and it was a perfect seventy degrees. The food smelled delicious, making her stomach rumble with hunger. She could get used to this. "So is this the treatment you give all the American tourists who stop by your café?"

He winked. "Only the beautiful ones."

The giggles just kept coming, but this one ended in an unladylike snort. She blushed. She wished she had Brina here. Including this, Audrey could count on one hand the number of times she'd gone on a date. Brina had a sixth sense when it came to men. She'd be able to tell if this guy was sincere or a player. Or, maybe not. Maybe all Sicilians were Latin lovers and equipped to sweep women off their feet.

At this moment, caught up in the beauty of the island and the warmth of present company, Audrey didn't really care.

Truthfully, Audrey had been fully focused on her career most of her young life. She never even dated, except for some casual hangouts with losers who were never worth a second date. And yes, she was getting older. Maybe that would soon pass her by. She wanted a family, and kids, and all that good stuff. But she'd never even gotten close.

In fact, this? With G? As innocent as it was, it was probably as close as she'd ever gotten.

Maybe as much as she wanted it, love wouldn't be in the cards for her.

She cringed, thinking of how she'd been with Michael a couple months ago, back in Boston. Michael had been her first big crush from high school. He'd barely looked at her, all through school, and yet he sent her one Facebook message, and she'd nearly started picking out wedding invitations.

That is, until she showed up at her high school reunion to find out he was already married. Not to mention, a drunk. All he'd wanted her for was a tumble in the coat closet.

That was a perfect example of her usual luck with men.

But this was different. G was here, in the flesh, gazing at her adoringly. It could be different this time.

Doesn't matter, Audrey. You always put the cart way before the horse. It's just a date, not a marriage proposal. Don't read too much into it. Have fun.

After lunch, their bellies full of something called *caponata,* a dish of eggplant, tomatoes, raisins, capers, and pine nuts that came in a close second to G's famous *ciambotta,* he bought her a creamy, delicious strawberry *gelato* from a stand, then took her hand and guided her down the street. At the top of the street, she had a perfect view of the looming, white-capped Mt. Etna. "It's active, right? When was the last time it erupted?" she asked him.

He laughed. "I think we are safe for today," he said, leading her past ruins of a small Roman theater. She climbed through the crumbling remains, admiring the old marble statues and ornate columned architecture.

When they emerged from the ruins, she blinked in the bright sunlight. "That was fascinating."

He called her attention to a gorgeous baroque-style cathedral, and a square with a magnificent fountain with an elephant atop it, a large obelisk protruding from its back. Considering all the baroque architecture surrounding it, the Egyptian- and Asian-inspired creature looked a bit out of place.

"*Piazza Del Duomo,*" he said, waving his arms about dramatically. He pointed to the ornate cathedral, with its double spires stretching into the sky. "Very famous. That there is the *Basilica Cattedrale Sant'Agata.* You like?"

She nodded. "It's nice, but... that fountain. It's strange, with the elephant, isn't it? What does it mean?"

He swung his head around to look at it. "Not everything has to mean something. Some things can bring joy just by existing. *Si?*"

Indeed, it was beautiful, and it did make her happy, for some odd reason. It was clearly very famous, from the number of tourists that were swarming around it. She loved being among them, having nothing else to do but take in the history and sights. "You're making me not want to go back," she said to him, only half-joking.

G laughed at her. "Ah, but Mussomeli has its own charm, no?"

"It does," she admitted. *It also has its own problems. And a to-do list a thousand items long.*

He must've noticed the crease on her brow, because he said, "Ah, Audrey. You cannot escape your problems by running from them. But you can press pause on them for a bit. Take them on when you are in a better frame of mind."

Right. If moving halfway across the world had told her anything, it was that. She'd left Boston mostly to escape her humdrum, monotonous life. But she'd only found different problems in Sicily. Life was messy. It had ups and downs. The best she could do was weather the downs so she could enjoy the ups.

Like this. Instead of dwelling on what was waiting for her at home, she needed to be more in the moment for times like these, so she could fully enjoy them.

She stood at the base of the fountain, gazing up at it. "Why an elephant?" she asked. "What's the story on that?"

"Ha, Audrey, you are always thinking. Okay, I will tell you. There are many theories on that. But my favorite is the simplest. The *elefante* with its trunk up is good luck." G presented her with a coin to drop in. "For luck!"

She smiled, took the coin, and dropped it into the clear water among hundreds of other coins sparkling in the abundant Mediterranean sunshine. As she did, she wished what she always wished for, on birthdays, at wishing wells, everywhere… health and happiness.

And when G took her hand again, she also added another wish.

This one, for love.

CHAPTER FIVE

"I'm going to throw up, I think," Audrey said to Brina as she clutched the phone and headed toward the vet center on opening day.

"What are you worried about?" Brina yawned. It was two in the morning in Boston, but luckily Brina was up doing a middle-of-the-night feeding. "You're a doctor, remember? You know your stuff. People are coming to you because you're the woman with the answers. And you have a bit fat degree and student loans out the butt to prove it."

"I know," she said, though at that moment, she had trouble remembering where the vet center she'd been fixing up was. When she got onto *Via Barcellona*, she was momentarily distracted by a rather large crowd gathered in the vicinity of her new office.

Weird, who's giving what away, I wonder?

As she approached, people turned to look at her, and the chatter died down. When she caught sight of a cute little terrier in the arms of an older woman, a cold breeze gripped her and sent a shiver down her spine, and it suddenly hit her.

"Oh, God," she mumbled into the phone. "I've got to go."

One thing she'd learned while living in Sicily was that the town didn't really get moving until late morning. Most people didn't start their day until ten, at least, and lunch hours lasted two. And yet that didn't stop nearly, oh, what looked like most of the town from lining up for her opening day at just before nine in the morning.

She ended the call as she crossed the street and spotted Orlando in the doors, waving to her. He seemed a lot more thrilled than she felt, that stupid, white smile plastered on his politician's face. "Nice turnout, eh?"

"Um …" She paused and looked at the faces of all the pets and their hopeful owners, then asked a stupid question: "Is this all for me?"

"*Si*, it's exciting! Everyone in town wants to meet the famous new veterinarian. I told you that you would be a welcome addition," he said, leading her up to the front stoop. He'd actually unrolled some tape across the front of the building. He handed her some scissors. "Let's get it going so you can get started!"

She took the scissors and opened them, now thoroughly discombobulated. Didn't these people know anything about appointments? She couldn't possibly see all of them at once. It would be like... havoc. Insanity. "I didn't realize... I mean, I won't be able to see everyone... I can set them up for appointments ..." Or at least, her receptionist could. If she had one.

"Of course, of course. We'll get it all settled when we get inside."

Oh, God. Could all these people *fit* inside? Weren't there occupancy limits? A horrible thought flashed through her imagination, some of them hastily constructed walls collapsing in a giant cloud of dust, and all the resulting lawsuits, as she brought the scissors to the tape, preparing to cut it.

As she did, she thought of her father. Her father always told her she'd make something of herself, that she had it in her to do great things. And now, here she was, opening her own clinic, with her very own name on it. Tears pricked at her eyes. *If only he was here to see this...*

"One moment!" Falco said, laying a hand over hers. He produced a bullhorn and began to give a long, winding speech in Italian, sounding rather like a car salesman. Occasionally, he'd point to Audrey and say *Dottore Audrey Smart!* and people would clap politely.

"*... il miraculo!*" he said with great gusto.

Wait. Did he just call her a miracle? She knew she was needed, but she wouldn't go that far.

"*... santo della nostra piccola città!*"

And now it sounded like he was calling her a saint. *Way to sell them, Orlando, but you might want to tone it down a smidge?* She smiled at the crowd, growing redder and redder by the second.

Most of them looked back at her with sad, puppy-dog eyes, similar to the creatures they held, as if Audrey held the key to their very livelihood. She shrunk back, scanning over their heads until she saw G heading her way, smiling and shaking hands with just about everyone he came across. He gave some man a big bear hug, nearly lifting him up off the pavement.

Well, thank goodness for G. At least maybe she'd have help.

People clapped mildly, and Falco said a couple more Italian words and looked at her. "Okay. Now."

"Now? Are you sure?" He nodded. She lifted the giant, unwieldy pair of scissors and cut, and someone in the front of the crowd snapped a picture. Falco went ahead and opened the door. When she stepped in, inhaling the smell of the freshly painted walls and newly waxed floors, she realized someone had set out a buffet of treats and beverages for both the animals and the adults. "Oh! You did this?"

He nodded. "Yes, it was in the advertisement. You must have food for these things."

"Oh." She wondered what else was in the advertisement she hadn't been able to read. Was she going to be expected to give a speech? Walk around, greeting the guests? Check out all these animals?

People came in and began to help themselves to the treats. She smiled at them all as Falco motioned them to the waiting room and greeted everyone warmly, like a true politician.

"Well, *Dottore*," he said, "looks like a success, eh?"

"I don't know. It's going to take a while to get through all these—"

G approached them then, smiling. "*Principessa!* Or should I say *Dottore* here?" He kissed her on both cheeks. "You are the star of the city today! Everyone who is anyone is here right now."

"I'm glad you're here, G," she said hurriedly, glancing around as the crowds began to pack the place. "I need someone to log all these customers in so I can start seeing them."

Falco shook his head. "No. No appointments today. Just free tours and refreshments. But they should be able to make appointments for a future date."

Audrey sighed with relief. "Oh, good. Tours? I can handle that."

"I am happy to book the appointments," G said with a smile. "Do you have an appointment book?"

"Yes. Thank you. It's at the receptionist's desk. At my old place, I tried to keep my Fridays free for house calls."

"All right. I will get to it right now!" he said with great excitement, making his way to the desk.

"Audrey, if you'd like, I'll give the tours. And if you stay in the reception area, if anyone has questions or would like to meet you, G can help translate." Falco suggested.

Another sigh of relief. Maybe this wouldn't be so terrible after all. "Yes! That's great!"

More relaxed now, Audrey went to the reception area, greeting customers and their pets. As she finished petting a little white kitten, she stepped to the desk to see a woman with dark hair, severely pulled off her face in a tight bun, and pointy-toed heels, standing there, watching her. She was one of the few people who was not smiling. Her lips, rimmed in bright red, were a perfectly straight line.

"Hello," Audrey said, smiling and offering a hand to shake. "Welcome."

"Dottore Smart, I presume?" She was so busy eyeballing every corner of the room with a critical eye that she didn't notice Audrey's outstretched hand.

"Yes. Hi. That's me. Nice to meet you." She motioned to the buffet. "Have you had one of those yummy *sfio*, um, *svia*—"

"*Sfogliatelle*," she corrected, rolling her eyes.

"Right. They're delicious. Flaky and melt in your mouth. From a bakery over on—"

"No. I don't much care for sweets. Give me a tour, please," she said brusquely.

Audrey dropped her hand and looked to G. She would've loved some affirmation that this woman wasn't as witchy as she seemed, but G was too busy negotiating another appointment for an old lady's pet rabbit. Then she looked for Falco, but he was nowhere in sight, probably leading another tour.

"Well, I can take you around, if you'd like," she said with a shrug. This woman seemed to speak English fairly well, so it wouldn't be a problem. "Come on back."

The woman's heels tapped loudly on the new tile floor, over the steady rumble of conversation, as she followed Audrey through the waiting room. Though in front of her, Audrey couldn't help feeling like the woman's eyeballs were mentally ripping apart everything they settled on.

"Here, obviously, is the reception area," Audrey said, motioning with her hands. "And this is the waiting area."

The woman ran a disinterested eye over it all and let out a snort. "Hmph."

"Do you have any pets?" Audrey asked the woman.

"No," the woman said simply.

Okay, then it makes a lot of sense why you're here, Audrey thought. She'd asked the question because it would've given her a better idea of how to direct the tour. But she decided she'd just give a more general tour. Maybe the woman was just interested in local businesses. "Okay, come this way. Are you from around here?"

"Yes, I've lived here all my life."

"Oh. Great. I'm from the United States. Don't really speak Italian yet. I've only been in Mussomeli a couple months. But I love it. The people have been so wonderful and welcoming, really making me feel at home. It's a lovely town."

The woman didn't offer any response to Audrey's word vomit. The creases in her face only seemed to deepen, making her even scarier.

All right, Audrey thought, turning toward the hall. *Tough crowd.*

She led the woman down the narrow hall, past the pictures of adorable puppies and kittens she'd hung just the other day. She smiled at them. Any pet lover would, because they were so darn adorable. But when she looked back at her guest, the woman didn't even seem to notice them. Her eyes were fastened on the floor, a pronounced wrinkle on the bridge of her nose. "What is that smell?"

Audrey inhaled. The scent of the wax and paint had dissipated; now it smelled like the animals that were in the reception area. Not like roses and fresh air and sunshine, but not terrible, either. "Oh, probably the pets."

"Is the ventilation in here up to code?"

"Yes. I'm sure it is. We had all of our inspections done last week." At the first door, she stopped. "This here is one of our exam—"

"I should hope so. It's a violation to house animals if the building isn't up to code. What was it originally?"

"A vacuum store. But—"

"Much different, a vacuum store from an animal clinic. You made all this progress in how long? Two—"

"One week, actually. I know, it was crazy. But I do have the paperwork from the inspection," she said. "We passed with flying colors. Anyway, here's the exam room. We have only one right now, but we'll be getting more, hopefully, as we grow."

When Audrey opened the door, the woman peered in. Her lips twisted, showing the pronounced lines in them that made her look older. *This is a woman not easily impressed,* Audrey thought, wondering what else she could do to gain her favor. "Prior to this, I was on staff at one of the premier veterinary centers in Boston, catering to all types of animals in the city, so I have several years of experience in managing city pets on a much broader scale than this, but I think it makes me well suited to—"

"Mussomeli has unique problems, though, compared to America," she spat out. "We are not rich like you Americans. We have different values."

"Yes… I suppose, but we all want the best for our animals. Don't we?"

The woman was silent, refusing to concede that point.

Okay, of course Falco does twenty tours and gets all the easy customers. I get the nudge from hell.

"Unlike America, we have many strays. Too many strays. And you help with that?"

"Yes, I do. I plan to. I haven't started yet, but—"

Impatiently, the woman ushered her on. "Go on with the tour."

"Okay. Sorry. And over here is the surgery." Audrey crossed to the other side of the hallway and opened the door, frowning when she noticed the garbage can in the corner was overflowing. She'd meant to take that out last night. Of course, she'd forgotten.

The woman's eyes seem to narrow in on it. She let out a small but significant cluck of her tongue.

"I know everything's a little haphazard. Like I said, I only started on this place last week, so we were under a time crunch to get everything done," Audrey explained, leading her farther down the hall. "So it's very much a work in progress. But it's operational, at least. And we'll address the issues as we go. We have separate kennel areas for the cats, dogs, and small animals, but unless they're ill, rather than caging them in kennels, we like to give them room to explore and interact. And of course, there's a little area outside in the back where they can get fresh ai—"

She frowned. "You're taking in the strays?"

Audrey nodded. "We plan to, yes."

"And where do you keep those?"

"Well, once they get a clean bill of health, they'll be in the kennels with the other dogs and cats, too. We'll have special hours and events for adoption in the coming weeks, with hopes that we can find them all good homes. But—"

"And if they're not adopted?"

"Well, we'll hope that they are. But in the event—"

"This is a poor village. People don't have the money to feed themselves, much less another mouth. Many of the strays once belonged to loving homes which had to let them go. So if they are not adopted? What do you do then?"

Audrey smiled. "This is a no-kill shelter. If they're not adopted, they stay here forever. They'll always have a home here with plenty of love. I'm planning to ask for volunteers to come in and give the strays love, whenever—"

"The streets are overrun with strays," she snapped, speaking over Audrey. "And if you start taking them in, it's only a matter of time before this place is, too. I give you a week, no more, before the place is full of mangy mutts with nowhere to go. Disease will spread among the animals, and it will be far too expensive for you to maintain. You have not been here long enough to see the massive stray problem we have on our hands."

"I agree. I've seen a little, but not everything. Yes, it'll be tight. There is a big stray problem in Mussomeli. I'd love if we could have the storefront next to this place, since it's empty, too, but we simply don't have the money to —"

"If you don't have the money, how are you going to feed all those strays?" she demanded, hands on her hips.

Audrey blinked. Why did this suddenly feel like an inquisition? "We'll have to ask for donations."

She laughed. "*Madre de dios*. Like I said, Mussomeli isn't a rich town. Most people here are struggling to survive. They don't have money for *donations*." She said it like it was a dirty word.

The tour was over. Sure, there was the stockroom and lunchroom in the back, but Audrey was worried her guest would go ballistic if she saw those, since the renovations hadn't touched them, their meager budget spent on the more important patient areas. She motioned to her to turn around and they walked back up to the front of the building. "Well, I do understand that, but all the expats moving here might. And someone needs to deal with Mussomeli's stray problem."

"Yes, that is true, Dr. Smart, but I'm not sure this is the best way to go about it. It's wasting money that can better be spent elsewhere. The streets downtown are so full of potholes and the fountain in the main square is crumbling away and no one fixes those, because the city doesn't have the money. Yet we have money to care for strays?" She shook her head. "If we don't get the common areas of Mussomeli taken care of, it'll turn away all those people who are thinking of moving here. They'll buy one-euro houses in other cities. You know, plenty of other cities are doing the program. Mussomeli needs to stand out to attract those who moved out back to it."

And Audrey thought Mason was a Johnny Raincloud. This person was unbelievable. Falco had told her it wasn't in the budget to give her more money *right now*. Now, Audrey wondered if Falco would *ever* have the money in the budget. She frowned. "Yes. I see what you're saying, but—"

She stopped when they reached the reception area and she noticed Mason, standing in the corner, scanning the area carefully, like he'd just entered a minefield. He focused with disgust on a woman who was feeding a cannoli to the tiny pug on her lap. Other than that, with his longish hair slicked back on the sides—likely he'd just showered—and his white T-shirt, he looked like a sexy greaser.

Johnny Raincloud or not, she smiled. He'd come.

When his gaze shifted toward her, though, that look of disgust didn't disappear.

In fact, it got worse.

Okay, I know we don't get along all the time, but what's that look all about? she wondered, scanning over toward G, who was deep in conversation with another one of his friends. The appointment book in front of him looked pretty full. Maybe he could be her permanent receptionist. He was darn good at it.

She almost forgot about the woman next to her until the older lady cleared her throat, loudly and obnoxiously. "You say you have had inspections? Where are your permits?"

Audrey turned to her, a little distracted. "Uh, permits?"

"Yes. You have permits, don't you? You need permits."

"Oh, yes. Sure. They're around. I think. Somewhere. It's been so much of a whirl—"

The woman let out a little huff. "They need to be posted. In the main area. Easily seen. You may do things different in America, but this is how we do things in Sicily."

"Oh." Audrey had them… somewhere. Probably in the mess of papers in the reception desk. "We were planning to do that when we—"

"See that you do." The woman crossed her arms. "It's code, and extremely important. You could be closed down today."

A sinking feeling settled over Audrey, as she realized the woman hadn't introduced herself. "Um, you know I'm Dr. Smart. But I don't think I caught your name?"

"Mimi Catalano. I'm on the council with Orlando Falco," she spat out, still looking around, her face pinched. Audrey had to wonder if she was mentally compiling a laundry list of complaints.

Mimi Catalano. Why does that name sound so familiar? "Oh. It's nice to—" She started to extend her hand but the woman pushed forward, toward the door, shoving her outstretched hand back.

"I will return to make sure these violations are taken care of," she muttered, and about-faced with dramatic flair, applying giant-framed black sunglasses to her face.

Take your time. Seriously, take ALL the time. Audrey stared after her, clenching her teeth hard as the woman sauntered away, scrutinizing the buffet with disgust.

When Audrey finally looked away, Mason was standing in front of her, still fish-out-of-water. "I was in the neighborhood, so I thought I'd stop by to see how things were going," he said casually. "But they can't be going that good, huh?"

So he remembered. She smiled at him. "No, actually, they're pretty good! H—"

"What did that old, black-hearted sea hag say to you?" he muttered, staring daggers at the woman.

Audrey blinked. Suddenly, the pieces fell into place. Now, she remembered exactly where she'd heard that name before. Coming out of Mason's pretty mouth. "Wait. Mason. Is that... Is she ..."

Mason smirked. "Yeah. She's the witch who shut down my renovation."

The words were still hanging in the air when there was a massive thud and a shriek. Audrey's head snapped to the buffet in time to see Mimi Catalano's feet, flying up behind the food table.

"Oh, my God!" she shouted, skirting around the table. She found the councilwoman lying, dazed, on her back, in what looked like a puddle of pee. "Are you okay?"

She reached out her hand to help her up, but Mimi scowled and took another man's hand. When she got to her feet, she peeled off her sunglasses and said something in Italian. Her back was soaked, and her face was red. And Audrey didn't think she could look any angrier.

"I'm sorry," she said. "An animal must have had an ..."

She trailed off when Mimi's hand went behind her back, and she must've felt the dampness, because her eyes went from angry to downright scary. "*Madre di Dios,* this place is a death trap!" she shouted, effectively silencing the entire room. Now, everyone was looking at her.

Audrey groped idly for some napkins on the table, not that they'd do much good, as the woman stormed to the door.

"You have not seen the last of me, Dr. Smart," she said, pushing her sunglasses up on her nose. "You can count on that."

CHAPTER SIX

When Audrey finally flipped the sign in the storefront from APERTO to CHIUSO, she leaned against the door and let out a sigh of relief as she scanned the empty waiting room, full of empty cups and plates and the normal debris a hundred or so pets would leave.

"Thank goodness that's over," she muttered to the ceiling. "I'm exhausted."

G poked his head up from behind the reception desk, where he'd been busy writing something in the appointment book. "I hope not too exhausted. You're going to be very busy soon, my dear."

She raised an eyebrow and peered over his shoulder at the appointment book. Sure enough, every available slot for the next week seemed to have been booked. "Wow."

He smiled. "What can I say? You were sorely needed here."

"I guess. Thank you. I couldn't have done it without you," Audrey said. "You're a natural at this."

"Ah." He waved the thought away, as if to say, *Think nothing of it.* "Turns out this is a lot like taking reservations during the dinner rush. I'm good at—how do you say—doing two things at one time."

She stiffened as a thought came to her. "Dinner rush? Wait, aren't you expected at the restaurant for dinner?"

"Nah. I get my business partner, Valentina, to cover for me today."

"Business partner?"

"*Si.* She handles my books and more. She's as stunning as she is smart. Customers like her more than they like me!" He chuckled.

This was the first she'd heard that he had one of those. And a stunning woman? Great. She was already intensely curious over Mason's "friend." *Well, really, Audrey, what about his asking you to tour the island with him meant that you were dating? He's a friendly man. Hugs everyone. Of course he has a stunning "business" partner, handling his affairs and "more."* She didn't need anything else to wonder about, so she shoved the thought aside. "Well, I really appreciate you taking time away from your business to help me."

"It's the least I can do. But unfortunately, I do have my own business to tend to, so I do hope you find help soon."

"Oh, of course! You were great. I couldn't ask for anything more from you."

"Maybe you get some volunteers? Young people love being with animals. I ask around."

"That would be great!"

He pushed away from the desk and started to clean up some cups and crumpled napkins that had been left around. The place was a bit of a mess, and needed cleaning if tomorrow it was going to be business as usual, but G had done enough.

She took the plates from him. "Oh, stop. You don't need to clean up this mess when you probably have one of your own in your restaurant!"

He flashed her his charming smile and winked. "I insist."

"And I insist you go! Please. You've done so much. Too much. I can handle this myself. You go home."

"All right, all right. If you say so. I was going to ask you if you wanted to come to the restaurant for dinner?"

She considered the offer, but after the news about Valentina, her heart wasn't in it. She shook her head. "Honestly, I'm exhausted." Not to mention that she'd nervously filled up on cannoli and *sfogliatelle* while greeting potential patients. "I'm just going to go right home after I clean the rest of this up and crash."

"So, there is nothing else you need before opening tomorrow?" He pointed to the first appointment for the next morning, which was at nine.

Actually, there were a few things. After Mason had dropped the bomb that Mimi Catalano, the same stickler who'd closed down his renovations, was now casting her critical eye around the vet center, Audrey had been more on edge than before. She'd been making a mental list to go through the place with a fine-tooth comb and make sure everything was up to code, starting with posting the permits visibly in the window. But she would get to all of that herself.

"Yes. I'm sure. Again, thank you."

He grabbed his skull cap and fixed it on his head, then turned to face her. "You need me to help tomorrow?"

She shook her head. "Oh, no. Really. I need to learn to deal with this myself."

"You can call me if you need anything."

"I will."

He put both hands on her shoulders and kissed both of her cheeks with great gusto. It wasn't exactly a romantic gesture, but then again, she was too tired to feel very romantic herself. She wanted to get home and take a nice, long shower, and maybe relax with a glass of wine.

Instead, after G left, she started to clean up the mess. She walked through the place, trying to make sure everything was spic and span. Each time she entered a room, she pretended she was Mimi Catalano, looking for fault. It was like walking on eggshells. The fact was, she didn't know what little thing would set the councilwoman off.

"It's fine," she finally said, yawning as she drew the storefront curtains closed, turned off the light, and stepped onto the front stoop. She twisted the key in the lock to make sure it was closed up tightly for the night, then turned to face the dark street. The sun had gone down hours ago.

She had barely taken the first step when she peered down and saw Nick. The little red fox looked up at her, as if expecting a treat.

She laughed. "Did you follow me? Have you been waiting out here all day, boy?"

He sniffed at the toes of her sneakers and wrapped his tail around her legs, his way of saying hello, I've missed you. She wasn't technically allowed to have a wild fox as her pet, but after helping Detective DiNardo of the Mussomeli police with his cat's problem, she'd been granted a special permit to keep him in her home. He'd been injured then, and needed her help. But now, she needed him just as much. Sure, she had made a few human friends, but Nick was the one who got her through many a lonely night in this new, strange town, thousands of miles from home.

Two months in Mussomeli, and Nick was already her favorite thing about the place. "All right, Nick, my boy, what would you say to a big bowl of kibble and a few app—"

Before she could finish the sentence, he jumped to attention, his ears perking up. Then he took off like a rocket down the street. Audrey shouted after him as he went, glimpsing a small black shape darting into a back alley, Nick at its heels.

A stray, likely.

She sighed. That glass of wine and her lumpy but comfortable mattress was calling to her, but catching and bringing in strays *was* her job, after all.

Taking a deep breath, she stepped off the stoop and followed her pet into the alley. It was predictably dark, and the alley itself was narrow, the floor of it curving in a V-shape so that she splashed through a small gully of water at its center. Grabbing her cell phone, she put on the flashlight and arced it out in front of her.

This is a sure way to get mugged in Boston, a voice inside told her. *Maybe even here, too. The brochures said it was one of the safest towns in Sicily, but they always say that, don't they? The truth is, you don't know what the crime rate is around Mussomeli.*

"Pssst," she whispered, passing a few back doors to Barcellona Avenue businesses and garbage cans. The pungent stench of spoiled food wafted into her nostrils, and her stomach turned. "Nick! Where are you?"

Just then, a cat screeched up ahead and another animal growled. She shined the flashlight toward the sound. Up ahead, the alley stopped at a chain-link fence. There was a black cat at its base, hissing at Nick, who was cornering it, trying to play ferocious beast. He growled again, louder and more menacing this time.

"Nick!" Audrey warned. "Give it up. You're scaring the poor little guy to death."

She moved closer to the cat, who hissed louder. Even in the dim light, she could already make out the telltale signs of mange on its coat.

"Poor thing," she said, wishing she'd brought some supplies with her. She reached into her purse and pulled out a spare dog biscuit that she always carried around with her. What she needed, really, was a cat carrier, someplace to put the animal so she didn't spread its disease.

She was just crouching to offer it to the cat when it suddenly lunged at her, jumping over her shoulder, its tail batting her cheek.

Audrey let out a yelp and fell backward onto her backside in a puddle of dank water. The cat gave her one last look, like, *You can keep your cruddy dog biscuit, fool,* easily scaled the fence, and slipped over the other side, out of sight.

Sitting there, shocked, soaked, and shivering, Audrey groaned. "Ow." She looked over at Nick, who seemed uninterested in her plight. "This is a fine mess you've gotten me in—"

Just then, one of the back doors flew open, spilling the pungent scent of garlic and a shaft of light onto Audrey's sitting form. A large rotund figure in a chef's toque took up most of the space in the doorway, shouting frantically in Italian. It wielded a broom at her.

"Sorry!" Audrey jumped to her feet. "I'm going!"

She scrambled back the way she came, not stopping until she'd reached the sidewalk on Barcellona.

Heaving a breath, she looked at her fox friend. "I think we'd better call it a night, Nick. No more animal chasing, at least until daylight. Okay?"

He simply turned toward home, intent on leading the way. Good. The last thing she needed was anything else to keep her from her wine and her bed.

Besides, today might have been busy, but tomorrow promised to be even worse.

*

There were a lot of things Audrey Smart loved about Sicily—temperate weather, quaint cobblestone streets, warm breezes that smelled of citrus and olives—but her possessed shower was not one of them.

"Oh, come *on!*" Audrey shouted as she twisted the hot and cold knobs to a pathetic dribble of water.

Her shower was drooling at her, which was actually one of the nicest things it had done for her thus far. In her not-quite-a-month living in a one-dollar house in Mussomeli, she hadn't once been able to get it to actually serve its purpose of giving her a nice, relaxing, hot shower.

"I hate you," she muttered at it.

She grabbed a wrench and lightly smacked one of the exposed pipes.

Suddenly, the drool became a torrent, nearly blasting her back against the tiled wall. Holding her hands out and pushing against the full force of the water as it drenched her, she made her way to the controls and twisted them. By then, she was thoroughly soaked, sneakers and all. Joy.

"Ow. And it looks like the feeling's mutual." She rubbed the back of her sore head.

It actually moaned in answer, so loud that Nick ran away whimpering.

"Aw, it's okay, Nick," she called. He was usually brave when the situation called for it, but it appeared the shower was just too much for him.

Funny, she'd thought that of all the rooms in her house, which happened to be one of the nicest in town—or at least, it *would* be, if she could get this show on the road— the troubles with this room were behind her. She'd added a new toilet, retiled, connected a new sink, repaired the crumbling hole in the foundation, and painted the walls a pretty burnt sienna. She'd thought she could mark a big check next to this room. Done.

Apparently not.

And she had about twelve other rooms to think about when this one was done, since this was one of the bigger homes in town, something she hadn't known when she bought it sight unseen.

Not to mention, absolutely zero in her bank account to finance the rest of the renovations.

Sighing, she tried again, following the directions Mason had given her. She made a few more adjustments to the antique bronze controls of the faucet, not expecting much. But the next time she twisted the faucet, she got just the right amount of pressure. She grinned. "Ta-da!" she said, smiling at Nick, who'd peeked his little red head into the doorway, as she breathed on her fingernails and buffed them on her Boston College T-shirt. "I know, I'm pretty awesome."

Nick seemed to nod adoringly. Sometimes animals were *such* better company than people.

She quickly turned the water off before her possessed shower could tell her otherwise.

Audrey grabbed her tools and went into the kitchen. The picture window let in the moonlight, slanting in between the tightly packed together rows of homes, but it also perfectly framed her neighbor Nessa, who was standing on the front stoop, directing a couple of beefy guys with a brand new white leather sofa. *"Dai! Mi fa cagare! Dio! Stupido!"*

Audrey had no idea what she was saying, but if it was like ninety-nine percent of what came out of Nessa's mouth, it probably wasn't anything nice. Audrey pitied anyone who had the misfortune of working for the woman, who was supposedly an internet celeb in the home improvement and interior design world and could afford to farm out most of her renovations to local contractors. Nessa's renovations had been going swimmingly, only because of her army of behind-the-scenes workers. Every time Audrey poked her head outside, she found something new to admire about the home across the street.

Not that she was bitter or anything.

Okay, maybe a little bit.

But there was something to be said about doing it all—or most of it—on one's own. Sinking blood and sweat and tears into a home would endear the place to her even more. Eventually, she'd be proud to invite guests here to stay, and all of them would admire her for the work she'd done. Maybe one day, even the shower would make peace with her.

Her phone started to ring. It was Brina, her big sister and best friend, back in Boston. She pressed the phone to her ear. "Hi!"

"Hey, so how was the clinic's grand opening?"

Audrey winced, thinking of Mimi Catalano's big spill. "Exhausting. Tomorrow's our first official day."

"You were supposed to call me to tell me how it went. I thought you died."

"No. And I promise I'll send you photos of the house the second I can. I'm slowly getting through things. Fixed the downstairs bathroom."

Brina didn't sound impressed. "I thought you already finished that."

"Minor setback," she muttered, twisting her T-shirt in front of her and wringing it out in the kitchen sink. "I fixed it *again*. Had to re-jigger it. It's all good. One room down, twelve more to go. Slow and steady wins the race. Right now, I'm focused on my clinic."

"If you're not going to send me pics of the house, at least send me pics of that young Italian stud who can cook."

She meant G. "I can't do that."

"Okay, then what about that egocentric American with abs you can bounce quarters off of?"

That was Mason. Yes, he had abs, and was so good-looking, it made her eyes hurt. He was one of those people who spoke constantly in double entendres, so she never could be sure if he was flirting with her. "Why do you care? You have Max. Your husband? Remember?"

"The bigger question is, why don't *you* care?" Brina asked. "I mean, you're single, eligible, middle-aged, and your biological clock is ticking away the seconds …"

Audrey moaned. Not this again. She'd had a semi-successful career in Boston as a veterinarian, but she'd also felt completely stifled. Like her life lacked all connection, all sense of adventure. This move out to Sicily had been her way of breaking free. But though her male prospects were slightly better on this side of the Atlantic, she'd actually been too busy trying to keep a non-leaking roof over her head to barely even think about romantic pursuits.

And… middle-aged? Ouch. She was thirty-two. Was that middle-aged?

She'd never heard herself referred to in those terms but she had to admit… Yes. Probably, it was. "Maybe you'll just have to come here and visit me."

Brina snorted. It wasn't likely, considering she had three young kids. Though Brina made it look effortlessly glamorous, she was very much the doting mother. It wasn't like she could drop everything and fly here on a moment's notice.

"Fine. I'll send you a picture of *something*. Soon. I promise."

"Abs. Please?"

Audrey laughed. "Seriously?"

"Sure. And see if you can make it into one of those 3D shots. Max is getting a little mushy around the center. Maybe I can give him something to aspire to."

"All right. You asked for it."

"Good. I'll be waiting."

"I've got to go. Like I said, I have the clinic to worry about."

And Mimi Catalano.

Inside, she felt her heart beating hard. She willed it to slow down. Mimi didn't matter. Her new vet practice was a reality, and her first real day on the job would be better. She couldn't wait to change some lives.

CHAPTER SEVEN

At nine on the dot, when she went outside to flip the *CHIUSO* sign back to *APERTO*, her first customer, a woman with a big, fluffy Bolognese named Fabio, was right on time for her check-up appointment.

Though he was a good boy, he shed clumps of fur all over the place as she gave him his examination and clean bill of health. She said goodbye to them, checked them out with little difficulty, helped them outside, and barely had time to sweep up before the next customer arrived, a quiet, goateed young man with a pet rabbit that wasn't eating properly.

"One moment," she said to him, holding up a finger as she grabbed the broom and the cleaning solution. "Please have a seat. Need to sanitize. I'll be back in a second."

I can do this, she said to herself as she scrubbed the exam room clean and swept up the rest of the hair. *Sure it would be nice to have a vet tech to help, and a receptionist, but I got this. It'll be fine.*

When she returned to the waiting room to find a boy there with a gray kitten and a man in a suit, she started to wonder.

"Um... can I help you? Are you two together?" she asked, gesturing with her arms to indicate what she was saying. *Please be together.*

The man shook his head and motioned to the boy to go first. Great, so that meant there were two more problems to deal with. She felt a flush climbing up the back of her neck as the little freckle-faced kid, who couldn't have been more than seven or eight, started to speak breathlessly in Italian. She couldn't understand a word of it.

"Um ..."

The man in the suit reluctantly filled in, looking rather annoyed to be kept waiting, since he kept checking the time on his cell phone. "The kitten's a stray. The boy found it in his backyard, and his mother told him to turn it in to you because you would know what to do with it."

"Um ..." She stared at it, looking decidedly not like the expert who knew what to do with it. "Oh! Thanks. Nice to meet another American!"

He looked at her like, *God forbid.* "I'm Canadian."

"Oh." She turned to the little boy and took the tiny furball out of his hands. "I'll take it from here. I'll make sure he's well taken care of. Thank you very much. *Grazie*."

The boy pouted, clearly reluctant to surrender the animal, so Audrey added, "Keep working on your mom. Maybe she'll let you come and adopt him once I've checked him out and neutered him."

The boy just stared blankly at her, then shrugged and headed for the door. She *really* needed to get some Italian lessons.

At least the man in the suit would be able to understand her. "Yes?"

He let out a huff of air. "I need you to come to the abandoned factory across the street from my place." He grabbed the pad off the reception desk as if he owned the place and scribbled something down, then tore off the sheet and thrust it toward her. "This is the address. There's a colony of cats living in the place and they're multiplying and it's only getting worse. They poop all over my doorstep. I need them gone. And soon."

A trickle of sweat broke out on her ribcage. "Oh. Okay. Well, after I get done with my appointments for the day, I'll—"

"I don't care. Just see that it happens soon." He turned on his heel and strode outside, nose already buried in his phone.

And he thinks Americans are bad. I thought Canadians were always happy and relaxed.

Audrey sighed. The slight man holding the rabbit in a carrier on his lap had been waiting patiently, and now he cleared his throat.

She went to welcome him inside but then remembered the kitten, who was now squirming in her hands and mewling softly. She held up a finger. "One sec. Let me just ..."

She dashed into the back and set the kitten down in the kennel that she'd designated for the felines. She gave him a bowl of water and a few pats, a couple of little toys to keep him amused, then pulled out one of her intake forms. She stared at the space that said NAME. "Let's see. I think I'll call you Chai," she said, scribbling the new name and date on the form.

She'd fill out the rest later.

Finally, she went out to the front again. She was about to call for the man with his rabbit when she noticed a small, nondescript cardboard box sitting in the reception area. At first, she thought the mailman had brought a package.

Then the box shook.

And shifted across the floor.

And yipped.

Oh no. She looked over at the rabbit man. "Did you see who …"

He scowled. She stopped. It really didn't matter. What mattered right now was that there were a bunch of strays in her lobby that would likely run rampant if she didn't get them into a kennel, and quick.

She pulled open the flaps to reveal a litter of six energetic, squirming mutts, likely crossed between a terrier and a pug, each one probably only a few weeks old.

Oh, cute! she thought, and then, right after: *Oh, boy.*

She dragged her hands down her face and smiled apologetically at her next customer, then lifted the box and scurried into the back again. This time, she let the pups go in the dog kennel together, and didn't bother filling out an intake form. She'd do that later. But the little guys were too cute. She couldn't help petting each one and thinking up names for them, as she usually did with strays. There was a chocolate one that looked like Biscotti, a white and brown one that looked like a Cannoli …

She kept thinking food names. Before she could wonder why, her stomach growled. No wonder. She hadn't had anything to eat at all today.

The phone in the lobby began to ring. *Just go to voicemail!* she thought frantically, and then wondered if she even had voicemail. Heart beating steady in her chest, Audrey finally tore herself away, muttering under her breath that she'd name the others later.

She checked her phone as she came back, out of breath and flustered. Great. She was a half hour late for the rabbit's appointment. G had really packed them into her schedule, giving her no breathing room at all. Not even a lunch. She'd probably collapse from hunger. Her fault, really, for not giving him better instructions. But if she was later and later with each appointment, she probably wouldn't need *Piazza Tre*—she might as well stay in the clinic and work there twenty-four-seven.

Finally, she smiled at the man with the rabbit. *"Scuzi,"* she said, looking over the appointment book. "Rinaldo? I apologize for the wait. You've brought your rabbit, Carota, to be checked out? He's having digestive issues?"

The man nodded in a way that made Audrey think he had no idea what she was saying. She motioned to the pet carrier and started to take it when the phone at the reception area began to ring.

She didn't want to put the poor man off any longer, so she swept up the phone as she peered in the carrier, doing a preliminary inspection.

"Dr. Audrey Smart," she said, as the bunny stuck his little twitching nose through the bars to sniff her finger.

At once, someone began to speak Italian. "Whoa. Hold on," she said, grabbing a pen. "I can't understand. Can you speak slowly?"

The person kept on speaking, getting faster, louder, and more annoyed; at least, Audrey thought. She tried to get a word in, telling the person to calm down, but it didn't work. Audrey had to pull the receiver away from her ear to avoid having it burst her eardrum.

When she could finally get a word in, she said, "I'm sorry. Do you need an appointment?"

She'd barely finished those words when a young, bearded man ran in, holding a bulldog in his arms. He was on the verge of tears as he shouted, *"Aiuto! Aiuto!"* And then he began to shout in incomprehensible Italian as well.

Wincing, she'd just begun to respond to the person on the phone when there was an audible click, and silence.

They'd hung up on her.

She placed the phone down on the cradle. "I'm sorry, sir. What is it?"

Through a series of hand gestures, she managed to find out that the dog had eaten something that he shouldn't have, and that he'd been lethargic all morning. She raced him back to the surgery and laid him on the cot. The poor thing. He was definitely in trouble.

As she stared at him, trying to take his vitals, he opened his mouth and let out a belch. Then he started to yak. He convulsed violently.

And he threw up a red, golf-ball-sized thing. It looked—and smelled—like an entire onion.

Audrey winced in disgust, as the animal jumped up on the table and began wagging his tail excitedly, pronouncing himself cured.

Okay, so that was that.

She checked him out again and said to his owner, "He's fine. He'll stay overnight. We'll keep him for observation," she added, pointing to the ground and then miming sleep. "You're lucky you brought him in when you did."

He nodded, even though she got the feeling he didn't understand that last part. "Ah! *Grazie.*"

She realized as she got to reception and he started to take out his Visa that she'd forgotten to give him the intake form. And she had absolutely no clue what to charge. This was something the administrative staff at Back Bay Animal Care took care of. She never had to touch the money at all. She handed him the form on a clipboard.

"Uh, can you just fill this out? And I'll bill you? Leave it here when you finish. *Grazie*. Thank you."

He nodded and began to fill out the form. Pulse pounding, she spun around the room and saw it filling with people and their animals. She then saw the rabbit, still sitting in its carrier. Its owner was now tapping his foot impatiently, and with good reason.

A parakeet shrieked something in Italian, adding to the cacophony of animal noises. Audrey was used to that sound—in fact, it was usually music to her ears. But right now, she had a major headache. Sweat beaded on her brow.

"Okay. I'm sorry for the delay," she said brightly. "First day. It's a little crazy."

"Hmm," he responded, as if he didn't care.

She grabbed the carrier and started to bring the bunny toward the exam room. "Let's get this little guy weighed and see what's going—" She stopped when she heard the front door creak open. "Oh, for heaven's sake!"

She whirled to the front and the sweat on her brow turned to ice.

Mimi Catalano stood in the doorway, those critical eyes of hers doing laps around the place.

Things weren't exactly in the condition she'd left them in when she'd done her inspection last night. Actually, far from it. There was still a pile of dog hair in the middle of the floor that she'd swept up, but hadn't yet disposed of. The reception area was now packed with people and their animals. Some animal had peed, a bright yellow puddle of grossness, right in the middle of the floor. Mimi's eyes landed on it, and her face puckered even more. She waved a hand in front of her face, because yes, the smell in the room was suffocating, and the place was too hot. The inspections were complete and Mason had said the HVAC was working, but apparently... not well enough.

Audrey took a deep breath. "Hello, Mrs. Catalano," she called, as confidently as she could. "It's a little busy here. First day. But if you'll—"

"Dottore Smart." She said it in a way that made Audrey freeze.

The woman skirted around the pee puddle as if it was hot lava. She was wearing a shiny red nylon tracksuit, oddly enough paired with matching red high heels and a lot of red, chunky costume jewelry. The woman didn't exactly strike Audrey as the gym-going type, and the heels didn't exactly convey comfort. Her makeup was thickly applied and a red hair clip was drowning amidst the pile of fried, permed hair atop her head.

No wonder Audrey hadn't realized who it was the first time she met her. *This* was the woman who Mason said he didn't discriminate against? She wasn't attractive in any sense of the word. Oh, she was made-up to the nines, but even so? She was downright *scary*.

"Yes?" she spit out, her voice cracking.

Mimi crossed her arms over her substantial chest and thrust her pointed chin in the direction of the window. "You're missing one of your permits."

"Oh?" She scanned the window. "I thought I had the—"

"You need the permit from the local businessmen's board. You only have the city and the federal papers."

"Oh! I have that. I must've just forgotten to—"

"And where's your certificate of insurance? You'll need it, considering hazards such as ..." She pointed to the puddle. "These."

Audrey scanned the reception area, where the full room was watching the back-and-forth as if involved in an engrossing tennis match. "Yes. Thank you. I have it. I can post it. Sorry. We had a few strays dropped off, and I'm still working through everything. It's been pretty busy, as you can—"

"It's not going to get any easier, I promise you that," she snapped, looking over the crowded waiting room. "Can I speak to you in private?"

Audrey nodded. It was better that way. She sensed an all-out reaming out coming, and she really didn't want it to happen in front of her new customers. "Yes. Why don't we step into my office?" She set the bunny down next to his owner. "Could you please—just, one moment, please?"

Now, he was no longer frowning at her. He was flat-out scowling. His eyes rolled to the ceiling and he muttered something, probably a curse word, in Italian.

"I promise. Just a minute. I am so sorry."

She thought about leading Mimi down the hall to her closet-sized office, but they'd have to pass all the strays, and her office was far from ready. Every surface inside it was packed with projects that still needed to be done, if only she could find the time. So instead, she opened the door to the exam room, since she'd cleaned it right before. Mimi's heels clicked severely on the tile floor as she stepped in behind.

Really, what she wanted to do was lead Mimi Catalano out the garbage chute, to the dumpster on the side of the building. But people would probably talk ...

The second Audrey closed the door, Mimi said, "It's busy now, but what's out there is only the beginning. You *need* to understand that. This is not child's play. And it is not America."

Audrey nodded. "Yes, but I'm planning to hire some help to—"

"With what money? *Dottore Smart.*" She shook her head like Audrey was a child who didn't yet understand the full ramifications of her actions. "The strays will keep pouring in. The sick animals. We have a big problem on our hands. And I'm afraid the only way to get it under control is not by taking these animals in. You simply don't have the money or the space to afford such luxury."

A sinking feeling coiled in Audrey's gut. "What are you suggesting?"

She shrugged as if the answer was obvious. "As I have been suggesting to the council for years, I think the simple, humane process of euthanasia will save these animals from any further suffering."

Audrey gasped. Her gut sunk even lower. "No. I'm sorry. I don't and won't do that."

The smile that came over Mimi's face was wrong. Sinister. "I think you'll find that it's the only way."

Audrey shook her head. "I will never find that. And I'm not going to even consider going down that road. It's hard now because I haven't gotten into a groove yet. But I do think it will get better. I think—"

"And if it doesn't? Will you consider euthanizing the strays?"

Audrey didn't skip a beat. "No. I'm sorry. Mussomeli would have to find another vet. I don't do that."

"Ah. That's a shame. Because I think if this problem continues, it's going to put a big blemish upon our revitalization efforts. We need to stop it as quickly as possible. You see?"

"I understand. And I'll do my best. But I—"

"I didn't want you, you see." She tapped her foot. "Falco, he's an old softy. You charmed him with your pretty, shiny hair and your smile. But you will not charm me. I put forward the motion to get in an animal control officer who would be skilled in eliminating these problems. He shot it down and recommended you. I said it was a waste of our money, but they agreed to give you a chance. I think it foolish. You? You'll never fix this problem."

"Animal control? You mean an animal murderer." She shivered.

"It's not murder if it is humane. So if I were you, I wouldn't get too comfortable here. You won't be here long," she said with that same sinister smile, opening up the door and strutting out.

Audrey stared after her, her mouth open.

It was only when the outer door closed and the parakeet started shrieking that she remembered the horrors that waited for her out in the reception area.

She'd show Mimi. She'd make this clinic a success and curb the stray problem, without killing a bunch of animals to achieve it.

Balling her hands into fists, she marched out to the waiting room.

But the chair where Rinaldo, Carota's owner, once sat was now empty. Every other chair was taken by someone, but her next appointment had given up on her and left.

Audrey sighed. A disgruntled customer on the first day. Perfect.

And with Mimi Catalano breathing down her back, threatening to close her down at every turn, she'd have to work extra hard to make sure there weren't any more.

CHAPTER EIGHT

"Don't worry, Henri," she assured the man with the iguana, her last client of the day, for the tenth time. He was an early-twenties hipster guy from Belgium who'd also bought into the one-euro house thing. He had an iguana who'd recently lost his tail during a renovation accident. Though there had been a language barrier—Audrey had about as much a grasp of French as she did of Italian—it was clear the man was beside himself with guilt over his poor pet. "Yes, he lost his tail, but you might not have done anything at all. Iguanas use their tails as a defense mechanism, sometimes dropping them themselves to give them time to get away from a predator. So it's fully natural."

The man scratched his goatee. "Eh?"

She tried miming losing a tail and shrugging, but then gave up. He'd never get it.

"Yes, and like I said, he's young enough that he might grow a new one in time. But larger ones might not, if they don't need the defense. They might simply bulk up. Again, all completely natural and nothing to worry about."

She mimed waving away, like *no big deal.*

"Eh," he said, seeming to understand. *"Merci beaucoup."*

Those were the kinds of clients she liked best. The kind with compassion, who saw animal lives as just as precious as human ones.

Unlike some witchy councilwomen, who believed animal lives could be done away with as simply as throwing out the trash. Councilwomen. Weren't they supposed to be looking out for the good of the town? What a joke. A town *needed* pets, if only to keep depression levels at bay. And was the councilwoman really trying to make her up to code so she wouldn't get into trouble? Audrey had the distinct feeling that if she were lying near death on a curb, Mimi Catalano would walk right past her.

She held the door open for him and waved at the carrier as the man stepped out onto the stoop. Coco, the iguana, stuck out its long tongue at her.

The second they turned away, Audrey bolted inside, turned the sign in the door to *CHIUSO,* and ran to the reception desk. She pulled stacks of papers and receipts out of the drawers, searching for that missing permit and the certificate of insurance. She found the permit right away, but the other item was nowhere in sight.

Things had calmed down by the end of Audrey's first day of work, but by then, the image had been firmly cemented in her head: Mimi Catalano, dressed like a witch, cackling as she hung a "Closed for good" sign in front of her building. Now, she could think of nothing else.

"Where in the world are you, Mr. Insurance Certificate?" she said aloud as she rummaged through the papers, imagining the field day Mimi Catalano would have if she didn't produce it.

After an exhausting search of all the drawers, she finally gave up and cleaned up the mess, readying the place for the following day. Before she left, she hung the lost permit in the window with the others, and closed the curtains tightly.

Again, *Piazza Tre* and a glass of wine were calling to her, but she couldn't. She knew she'd never be able to relax with the insurance certificate missing and the scepter of that woman hanging over her. *I'll get you, my pretty. And your little fox, too!*

So instead of turning right to head home, she turned left, toward the center of town. She skipped across the narrow street, past the old marble fountain, thinking of how she'd made a wish in the elephant fountain with G. For luck, and for love.

So far, neither of them had really presented themselves.

If anyone could help her, it was the man who'd gotten her into this. Her benefactor. Though he hadn't done much for the renovation except supervise, he was an animal lover, and a friend. He'd help her with the paperwork. Or at least, he might be able to get his fellow councilperson to lay off for a little bit.

The building was sandwiched between older ones, and had gothic, Roman columns in front of it and a long sprawling staircase. A street musician sat on the bottom stairs, playing some song on his acoustic guitar and crooning, as a little girl danced circles in front of him.

Audrey had gone to the municipal building to file for the permits, so she knew where to find Orlando Falco's office. As she walked through the grand hallway, she almost expected Mimi to sweep in on her broom, doing some fancy skywriting in the air. *Surrender, Audrey!* But the place was nearly empty. Much of it was already closed for the night.

When she reached Falco's office, she sighed. The door was closed. Of course. She'd have to try to get in touch with him when—if—her schedule ever allowed it.

The moment she took a step to the exit, a door behind her creaked open, and a voice said, "Audrey?"

She turned to find Falco approaching her in his dapper suit, briefcase in hand. With his snow-white hair, lean, six-foot frame, and Whitestrips smile, he looked every bit the dashing politician.

"Oh, you're here," she said.

"Yes, I was just on my way home. Busy day. How are you? How is the clinic? You must pardon me, I meant to get over there, but my schedule has been busy," he said, motioning her to walk with him.

As they walked together toward the exit, their footsteps echoing through the massive halls, she said, "Well, it's going fine. But I seem to have lost my certificate of insurance."

"Oh?" He stopped. "You applied for that. I'm sure I delivered it to you in that envelope. It's a sticker. Gold. This big." He held out his hands to form the size.

"Ah, is it? I thought I was looking for a paper. I think I have that." In fact, she was sure she'd seen it in the drawer. She let out a sigh of relief, but her gut still felt uneasy.

"Yes. Just affix it to the front door and you should be fine. Glad I could help," he said, holding the door open for her. "Have a good—"

"Actually, there's something else."

He paused. He looked tired, like he'd had a long day and just wanted to get home. *Join the club, buddy.* "Yes? Have you run into any problems?"

"Well, yes. You see …" She paused, trying to choose her words carefully. In the event they were friends, *This witch is trying to close down the clinic* probably wasn't the best way to open.

"Ah, but that's because you're new to the area. All new businesses experience growing pains. A few more ads in the paper, and you'll have more appointments than you know what to do—"

"No, that's not it," she explained. "I'm actually really busy. I haven't even been open two days and the kennel is almost full. I really would like to hire a couple helpers, if you know of anyone. An assistant, at least. But that's not what I wanted to—"

"I'm not sure if that's in our budget, but—"

"It's okay. I understand. It's nice to have but not possible now. That's not the main issue." He looked as though he was going to cut her off again, so she quickly blurted, "Mimi Catalano."

His expression changed at once, not exactly to disgust, but something like it. No, they *definitely* weren't friends. "Yes? What about her?"

"Well, she stopped by today. And yesterday, while you were busy giving tours at the Grand Opening. She told me I was missing the permits, but then she went off on a bunch of other things. I'm guessing she never was really a fan of the clinic?"

He frowned. "No. Unfortunately. She's been difficult about it from the start. She had her own ideas of how to deal with the stray problem."

"Right. She thinks catching and keeping strays is a waste of time and money. She wanted to hire an animal control officer and have them euthanized," Audrey said, voice rising, getting more and more worked up as she thought about it. "I told her in no uncertain terms that if that's what this town is looking for, I'm not the veterinarian who will carry those plans out."

"I understand, I understand," he said, holding out his hands in effort to calm her. "And by no means do all the members of the council want that. But yes, I admit that she's pushing for it, and she's rather one to make a big stink about it. She's quite the piece of work."

"She's not just making a stink, Mr. Falco. She vowed to close the place down if I didn't walk her line."

They were now at the front of the building, at the bottom of the steps. He looked away, down the empty street, and muttered something under his breath. "Dr. Smart. I'm sorry if she was difficult with you. But please, don't worry yourself unnecessarily. I will have some words with her, see if I can smooth things over some."

Audrey smiled. "You will?"

"Yes. At the earliest opportunity. I promise you, I will not let her do anything to close the clinic down. I—and many other people in this town—know that you and that place are a godsend. You must believe that."

She sighed with relief. Short of landing a house on Mimi Catalano and her broom, that was the best she could hope for. "Thank you. That would be great."

He checked his watch. "I must be going. I'll stop by later this week. I promise. Have a good night."

He turned to walk up *Via Barcellona*, and she went the other way, back toward her clinic. She stopped there, went inside, found the insurance certificate—a gold sticker, of course—peeled off its backing, and placed it in the window, near the other paperwork. Good. Now she was official.

But with Mimi Catalano in the picture, she had to wonder if she would be able to stay that way for long.

CHAPTER NINE

The following morning, fighting off nightmares of Mimi Catalano cackling like a witch as she flew in on her broom, Audrey burrowed under the covers, trying to fight the rising sun, which was pouring its rays over the bedroom. *Just five more minutes,* she told herself.

Then it happened.

BANG! BANG! BANG!

She'd grown used to the construction racket happening all over the town. When Nessa, across the street, had moved in with an army of construction workers, they'd made enough noise to wake the dead. But this sound was different.

Nearer.

She pulled a blanket off her head and looked over at Nick, who was sitting on the edge of the bed, ears perked.

BANG! BANG! BANG!

It was coming from downstairs. Someone was banging at her door.

She pushed out of her bed, wiping the sleep from her eyes. The last time this had happened, it had been a police detective, wanting to question her about her alibi in the death of a certain project foreman. Why did the people of Mussomeli seem to think it was okay to bang on people's doors at ungodly hours of the morning? At least, this time, she wasn't a suspect in a murder investigation.

Scuffing into her slippers and throwing on a fluffy chenille robe, she navigated her way down the stairs and threw open the door to see a pale nightmare in purple, with red-rimmed lips.

Mimi Catalano.

Audrey took a step back as the woman took a step forward, arms akimbo. "Well?"

"Um ..." Was that a question? "I was just about to make some coffee. Can I get you some?"

The woman let out a sigh and tapped her heel impatiently. Evidently, from the way she was made up, she'd been awake for hours. She was wearing heels with a track suit again—this time, purple. She said, "Don't try to sweet talk me. I told you to save that for Falco. You know why I'm here."

She didn't have an exact idea, but it seemed a good guess to reason that it was something about the vet clinic. Something that she'd done *wrong*, likely. Unless Mimi was now here to shut down her own renovation at *Piazza Tre*, not that much renovating had been going on lately. "Actually… can you be a little more specific?"

Across the street, a door slammed. Audrey looked over Mimi's shoulder at Nessa, who was stretching for her morning run, a sly little smirk on her face. "What did you do this time, Audrey?"

Audrey scowled at her.

It was a question that Nessa hadn't expected an answer to, since she started to skip into her run. But Mimi whirled around and said, "She was missing the required permits to operate her business."

Nessa, who never met a scandal involving Audrey she didn't like, slowed to a stop. "Really? That's interesting." She tutted.

"No, it's really not," Audrey muttered, motioning to Nessa to keep running. She looked pointedly at Mimi. "And I'm not missing the permits. They're in the window. I put them there last night. Even the certificate of insurance."

"I was just there. I didn't see them."

So she was going to fight her to the death on this? At least this time, Audrey knew she was in the right.

Before she could respond, Nessa came closer, still tutting. "I don't doubt it. I'd keep a close eye on her, if I were you. She's a shifty one. I said it ever since she moved in. Always peering out the windows, *snooping*. And my foreman was *killed* because of her." She said it in a conspiratorial whisper, like the two of them were old friends. "Yep, it's true."

Really? "Um, Nessa. I didn't kill your freaking foreman. Someone else did. Remember?"

She stared daggers back at Audrey. "Maybe someone else pulled the trigger, but you *drove* him to his death. All that complaining you did." She sighed at Mimi. "I had to hold off on my own renovations for an entire week! Can you believe that?"

Oh, the tragedy. Meanwhile, it was Nessa's accusations that had almost put Audrey in prison for life.

She looked at Mimi. "Mimi. Please look again. Because I know—"

"You're insinuating I need to have my eyes checked? I looked. Twice!" She pulled a phone out of her bag and thrust the display under Audrey's nose. It was a photograph of the storefront window for the clinic. A couple of the permits were visible, but sure enough, the others were partially obscured by the curtain she'd drawn before she left.

"Oh. Well, I see the problem now. They're there. It's just that the drapes are in the—"

"They must be visible. At. All. Times!" she barked, her face reddening. "I told you that. I'm sure I told you that."

"You probably did," Nessa said, butting her head in again. "She isn't very good with the details. Just look at her house."

Audrey frowned. What was wrong with her house? All right, she wasn't a regular Chip and Joanna Gaines from *Fixer Upper* like Nessa, but she had some sense of style. She just hadn't been able to flex those muscles much, with the clinic. "I'm sorry. I'll go and fix it. Right away. Well—" She looked down at her fluffy robe. "Once I get read—"

"Right away. This is a huge violation. You could be fined if a code enforcement officer saw it."

So the woman wanted Audrey to traipse downtown wearing her bathrobe and slippers to take care of this issue? Audrey could only stare at her. When Mimi matched that stare, clearly expecting her to get moving ASAP, Audrey threw up her hands. "I have to get changed. Fifteen minutes isn't going to kill anyone," she snapped, trying her best to keep the hard edge out of her voice.

When Mimi Catalano snorted and said, "We'll see about that," Audrey had just about reached her limit.

Nessa jogged off, laughing. Before she rounded the corner out of sight, she called, "I wouldn't take her word for it! Shifty with a capital S!"

Audrey rolled her eyes. She gritted out, "I promise. I'll take care of it right away. Anything else?"

Mimi started to lift her nose in the air and stomp away, when something behind Audrey, near her feet, caught her eye. Shock dawned.

"*Madre di Dio!* What is that?"

If Audrey didn't know any better, she'd think Godzilla just appeared in her kitchen. It was that awful. Nessa had already rolled her eyes and remarked that the gingham curtains Audrey had chosen for the kitchen window were "so folksy and quaint, perfect for someone like you." So now she was going to have to withstand more criticism of her decorating choices?

Steeling herself, she followed the councilwoman's line of sight, to Nick.

Oh, right.

Of course she'd have something to say about that one.

"Uh, he's a …" She couldn't bring herself to say what he was. Likely, Mimi Catalano didn't care about it anyway. "I do have a license for him."

"You do? Who authorized that?"

She didn't want to throw Falco under the bus, but right now, she didn't see any choice. "Orlando Falco."

Her mouth hung open for a few seconds before she spoke. "He authorized you to have a wild animal living in your house?"

Oh, no. This could be bad for Falco. Very bad. "Actually. Um, it's not a wild animal."

Mimi leaned it, inspecting it closely. "It looks like a—"

"Fox? I know, I know." She tittered nervously. "People always say he looks like one. But Nick is a dog. A mutt. He's um, part chihuahua, part Shiba Inu."

Mimi's mouth moved, going over the words Audrey had just said, but for once, no sound came out. It was like she was taking Nessa's advice and trying to determine if this was just another "shifty" play Audrey was pulling on her. Finally, she said, "It's not wearing its license."

The truth was, Nick hated wearing that thing. He'd chewed on it the last time she'd slipped it around his neck. "Yes, but I do have one. It's—"

"This isn't America. We have rules here that we expect our residents to abide by. You seem intent on disobeying the rules of this town, and we can't have foreigners coming in and doing as they please. If that creature—whatever it is—is found to be in violation again, I'll see that it's taken in by authorities and disposed of."

Audrey's jaw dropped. "Disposed of?"

"Yes. You heard me."

"What authorities?" Audrey said, her voice cracking. The woman had to be bluffing. There were no authorities to deal with the stray problem, no animal control office, which was why it'd become such a big problem to begin with.

Mimi simply shrugged and turned away. "Fine, at the very least, I will have the license revoked for your inability to follow our laws. Dottore Smart, I'm just trying to ensure that the town's rules are followed. I'm not the bad guy here."

Audrey watched her walk away, her cheeks flushing and her hands shaking at her sides. *That's funny. Because you sure sound like it.*

She closed the door and looked at Nick. Then she went to the kitchen drawer above the washing machine, her designated "junk drawer," and pulled out the license that Orlando Falco had given her for the keeping of Nick. The little circular emblem on a nylon collar was supposed to put an end to this kind of problem.

Already knowing the outcome, she hesitated for a few moments. Then she crouched in front of Nick and tried to put it on. As expected, he shrunk away against the wall, then skirted to the side, dashing into the bathroom. When he got there, he glanced back at her, like, *That again? I thought we had an agreement. You have destroyed my trust.*

She sighed. This was nothing new. When she first got the license, she'd tried to place the collar over his neck for hours. But he'd constantly slipped away. At one point, she'd managed to get ahold of him and put it on, but he'd whined like a baby well into the night, until she'd been forced to remove it, and found it nearly chewed to pieces. At that point, she'd decided it wasn't important.

He was hers. It was legal. That was all that mattered.

Now, it felt like a life or death thing.

"Come on, Nick," she called, following him. "You need to wear this."

She went into the bathroom, not wanting to corner him and make him suffer, but seeing no other choice. But the moment she stepped into the little room, she sighed. The room was empty, and the window over the toilet was open.

He was gone.

"Nick!" she called out, but of course, there was no answer. For a moment, she considered running after him, but work was calling, promising another busy day. And she had to make sure it was perfect.

CHAPTER TEN

Audrey rushed into work. The second she opened the door, even before she flipped the APERTO sign, Audrey took care of the permit problem. All it really took was a two-second job, moving the curtain to the side. Nothing worth getting steamed about.

There, she thought as she made the motion with a dramatic sweep of her hand. *Hope it is up to your high standards, Catalano.*

Then she went into the back and took care of all the strays. It was only her second day on the job, and she had eight of them, six dogs and two cats. She'd named them (yes, mostly after Italian food), given them check-ups and treatments and plenty of cuddles and exercise, filling her cup with the animal love that helped zap away all the negativity she was feeling for a certain councilwoman.

When she went to the door to officially open for business for the day, she peered up and down the street.

No Nick.

She twisted her hands. He'd be back. She was sure of it. He loved to run about all over town, but he always came back to sleep in her bed at night. And even without his license, he was smart and nimble enough to avoid the likes of Mimi Catalano and any "authorities" that might try to capture him.

At least, she hoped.

Thankfully, the day was much less hectic than the one before. Her first appointment was a simple check-up, and the second appointment didn't show, which gave her time to catch up on her billing and paperwork. While working the books, running the numbers, she decided that if she kept bringing in paying clients at a hefty pace, she should be able to swing boarding the strays and make a bit of a profit so that she could feed herself. If she worked overtime and weekends, she might even be able to hire a receptionist.

As for where she'd get the money to continue with her renovations, well… she'd just have to be really thrifty, creative, and do things slowly.

Very slowly.

As sat at the reception desk, checking her upcoming appointments and waiting for her ten-thirty appointment, the phone rang.

She picked it up. "Hello, Dr. Smart Veterinary, can I help you?"

"Dottore Smart?"

She knew that voice. "Yes... Mr. Falco?"

"That's right."

From his tone of voice, she could already tell it was bad news. "Is everything okay?"

"It is," he said. "Well, to tell the truth, it could be better."

Uh-oh, she thought. *Here it comes.* "What is it?"

"Are you busy tonight, after your shift at the clinic?"

She stiffened. Was he asking her out on a date? Wasn't he married? And like, thirty years her senior? Even though he was handsome and distinguished, she hadn't checked his ring finger, because, well, he was old. At least sixty. But maybe that was how these Sicilian guys rolled. "Well—"

"There's a council meeting tonight at seven PM. At the municipal building. I think you should be there."

"Oh." She let out a giggle, relieved. But then the full weight of what he was saying crashed down on her. "Uh, why?"

"I just received the agenda. And it seems that Mimi Catalano is proposing a new tax that would be of interest to you. It's a tax on anyone who takes in stray animals, and a pretty hefty one, at that."

"What? Are you kidding me?" Audrey shouted into the phone.

"No. I'm sorry. She doesn't take it lightly when her proposals are rejected, and when she finds something to target, she goes full-bore. Apparently, she's targeting the clinic."

No, she's targeting me, specifically, Audrey thought, staring at the Excel budget spreadsheet she'd just compiled for the clinic. With a *hefty tax* for harboring strays, she might as well kiss the idea of a receptionist, or of eating anything other than beans and rice, goodbye. "That won't pass, will it? You have friends on the board that voted in my favor before, right?"

"I don't know. It's ludicrous, of course, but Mimi has a lot of fans on her side. She's been known for steamrolling opposition and getting these things done. I'll be pushing back, of course, but it really would help to have you there, to put a face on how this will damage your business."

Audrey gritted her teeth. "Don't worry. I'll be there."

She hung up the phone and her gut twisted. *And I'll tell Ms. Catalano exactly where she can shove her stray tax.*

*

"And she actually showed up at my house at an ungodly hour of the morning!" Audrey babbled to Mason as they walked into the municipal building later that night. "Can you believe that?"

Mason shook his head in response, as he had been doing for the past ten minutes during the walk over, as she unloaded all the injustices Mimi Catalano had thrown at her. The more she spoke, the more riled up she got. No, she wasn't really planning on telling Mimi where to shove her stray tax… at least, before. Now she was so fired up, she wasn't sure she could trust herself to behave in a ladylike manner.

"It just… ugh!" She shook her fists. "The nerve. Am I right?"

"Yeah."

Audrey looked at him. He was remarkably calm for someone who'd been a Mimi Catalano victim. She could feel her heart rate skyrocketing off the charts. "Yeah? That's it? Don't you have anything else to say?"

He shrugged. "I don't know. Are you going to let me say it?"

True, she had been kind of talking over him the whole way over. But she'd been stewing all day, and now she finally had a sounding board. And every time she thought she was done, she remembered another mean thing the woman had done. "I'm sorry. Go ahead."

"Like I said. She's a—"

"A total witch, right?"

Mason nodded and gave her a warning look.

"I'm sorry. Continue."

He shrugged. "And, well, yeah. She's—"

"Got a lot of nerve, right?"

He pressed his lips together. "A lot of nerve."

"I know, right?" she blurted. "Totally."

She looked at him, waiting for more. The man was one of few words.

"A *total* witch," she filled in, as he grabbed her arm and led her down the hall, their words echoing through the open, marble corridor.

They were at the doors to the conference room, and Mimi Catalano was there, sitting on her throne up high, on a dais in front of rows of chairs, along with the other council members.

"Remember," he whispered to her. "Calm. If you're going to address them, don't let your emotions take over. Be civil. Don't attack her."

Audrey nodded as she scanned the room. Other than Orlando Falco, who waved at her, it was mostly strangers. But the room was nearly packed. "I know. I won't."

They each grabbed a copy of the agenda and found two seats together in the back of the room, and sat down to wait for the meeting to start. Audrey tapped her foot nervously until Mason clamped a hand down over her knee.

"Relax."

"How can I relax?" she said, pointing to the paper. She couldn't read much of it, but one thing stuck out to her. She read it over and over again. "I think this says fifteen percent. That's how much she wants to charge me! If I get hit with this tax, I'm going to be sunk!"

"You'd better cool it, girl, otherwise you're going to have something a lot more serious than that tax to worry about. That vein on the side of your head is about to explode."

She reached up and felt it. It was just a little bump at her temple, but Mason was right. If she didn't calm herself, she was likely to blow a gasket. She needed to settle down. She took a deep breath and scanned the faces of the people seated around the room. "Who are all these people? You think they're all pet-haters like the witch?"

He gave her a disapproving look. "Boston. Cool your jets."

"All right, all right."

He clamped his hand down on her knee and she realized she was bouncing it again. This time, he didn't let go. Ordinarily, she would've been excited by the touch, but it wasn't a nice, sweet gesture. It was a *Get yourself together before I smack you* kind of thing.

Finally, the meeting began. Most of it was in Italian, so Audrey didn't know what was going on. But she couldn't help zeroing in on Mimi Catalano. Though she couldn't understand her words, it was easy to read between the lines with her body language. The woman was loud, interrupting people. She had something to say about every subject, dominating the discussion. She rolled her eyes and gave people accusing stares, like they were lesser beings.

The woman was worse than a witch. She was an evil-spirited bully who fought anyone who didn't go along with her ridiculous demands.

By the time Orlando Falco looked at Audrey, her skin was crawling, and she had so much pent-up indignation that she very well could have gone up to the mic and unleashed a torrent of curses at her opponent.

He said something in Italian, and then added, "Dr. Smart, a recent transplant from America, recently opened Mussomeli's only veterinary clinic. She is here to give a statement regarding Councilwoman Catalano's proposed tax increase. Dr. Smart?"

All eyes turned to Audrey as she stood and made her way toward the microphone in the center aisle. She could feel Mimi Catalano's disdain on her, but she avoided eye contact. When she reached the podium, she pulled out a slip of paper she'd written her thoughts on and unfolded it. Then she said, "Thank you, Mr. Falco. I've devoted my life to the care of animals, and when I moved to this beautiful town, I was excited to be tasked with the responsibility of caring for its growing stray population."

Pausing briefly between sentences to allow Falco to translate, she glanced over at Mason, who seemed to be relaxing now, satisfied that she wasn't going to fly off the handle.

"There is a growing stray problem in Mussomeli. Many of the animals have disease and are severely malnourished, scavenging where they can for scraps of food. But it doesn't have to be that way. My clinic caters to the strays. It's a no-kill shelter, which means we keep the animals there, give them food and medication, and hold them until they're adopted into a loving home. But as you can imagine, despite scrimping and saving to ensure our dollars are spent wisely, our budget is very tight."

At this, she ventured a glance at Mimi, who was staring at her over the rims of her reading glasses, the top of one red-painted lip raised higher than the other, in a pronounced snarl. Just as expected.

"This tax would not only devastate my business, it would impede my ability to care for these animals properly. And these animals deserve compassion, not extermination. I believe I can turn this stray problem around with the resources I've been allowed, if given the time and support, but this tax would make my efforts all but impossible. I understand that Ms. Catalano thinks strays should simply be done away with, euthanized, but I think that is inhumane and unnecessary. I received my license to operate in Sicily a little over three weeks ago, and only just started to work on the stray population. I ask, actually, I beg the council to reconsider supporting this measure until the full results of my efforts can be realized. And—"

"*Grazie*, Dottore Smart," Catalano snapped.

"But I'm not finished," she said, holding up her paper. "I still have—"

"Yes, *Dottore*, your concerns are duly noted," the councilwoman muttered, flipping through the papers in front of her. "But we have a very busy agenda and have to keep things moving along."

"But I have a lot more to say on this subject! And you—"

"Dottore ..." she warned.

"This is a disgrace!" Audrey held her notes up. "You're deliberately letting your personal opinion of me and other expats interfere with your job. I deserve to be—"

"Submit your paper to us and we'll look it over," Catalano said, monotone, now not even looking at her.

"All right. Thank you," Audrey muttered, glaring at her.

She turned and went back to her seat as Falco finished translating. When she sat down, Mason leaned in. "Impressive. I really thought you were going to call her a witch to her face."

Audrey whispered, "I held back on the *Screw you, Mimi,* just for you. Do you think I did okay?"

He nodded, and was about to say something when suddenly, someone on the other side of the room jumped to his feet and began to yell something in Italian.

All heads swung to the man. He was bald, but with a heavy black beard, and his skin was bright red. As he shouted, spittle flew everywhere, and he gesticulated wildly, mostly shaking his fist in the direction of the council. Now, that was impressive. And gutsy. He was acting exactly like the person Mason feared Audrey would be.

Audrey leaned in to Mason. "Whoa, what do you think he's saying?"

Mason didn't answer, so intent was he on the man. Some members of the council tried to calm the man down, but he spoke over them, his voice growing louder and louder. People nearest the aisle shifted to the side to avoid getting smacked by his crazily gesticulating hands. Talk about a bulging vein—there was one long, purple vein on the side of the guy's neck that looked like it was about to spring a leak. Near the back of the room, a security guard advanced toward him, warily waiting for him to make the wrong move.

"Someone really pissed in his Cheerios," Audrey murmured as the man began gesturing to her. "I wonder—"

"Shh," Mason said, studying the man closely.

Audrey blinked. "Wait. Can you understand him? Is he saying something about—"

"A little. Now shush, girl," he said, not looking at her. "I'd understand more if you'd be quiet."

The man finished his rant, and Mimi Catalano had the nerve to roll her eyes. Then she said something back, in a condescending tone.

"Ugh. I could wring her n—"

"Shh," Mason whispered again, under his breath. "You wanna know what he's saying? Shush."

The conversation switched to Falco, who said something else. Audrey eyed the man across the way, who'd slumped into his chair, arms crossed, a scowl on his face. He was clearly not happy. *"Grazie,"* Falco said, and then there was a pause, and a switch to the next item on the agenda.

"What happened?"

Mason leaned in. "That was interesting. They're tabling the vote until next week."

"Oh."

He started to stand. "Want to get out of here?"

Apparently, since he wasn't allowing her to speak inside, she'd have to wait until they were out of the conference room. She stood up eagerly and followed him past the crowd and out the door. The second the door closed behind her, she said, "Well? What else was that scary guy saying?"

"Who? Mr. Clean? From what I can tell, he's a local animal lover and pet owner. And he was defending you, actually."

"Oh. He was?" He seemed so angry.

"Yeah, but he was pretty pissed off. He said that Catalano was always trying to shutter small businesses and then he called her a few names that I won't repeat to you, since you're a lady," he said with a wink.

"Thanks. Things got pretty heated." They started to walk back toward the building exit when she said, "I didn't even know you spoke Italian."

"A little."

"You don't know much Italian, but you do know the curse words? Huh."

He smirked. "Yeah, well, I learned the most important stuff first. I've been taking an online class in my free time. Trying to get better so that when people come visit me, I don't look like a total dumbass showing them around."

Right. He hadn't said much about the mysterious *guest*, but in Audrey's mind, she was probably blonde, with deadly curves, double-comma Instagram followers, and a lucrative sponsorship contract for some hot cosmetics brand.

She pushed open the door into the night. It was dark by now, and the air had an autumn-like chill in it. She shivered and tried to throw on the sweater she'd brought. Mason held it so she could find the second arm hole. He might have been a total nudge, but deep down, he was a good guy. "Thanks. And thanks for coming with m—"

She stopped when she caught sight of a red blur, dodging between the parked cars on the curb, heading her way.

"Nick!"

He dashed onto the curb and hopped into her arms.

"Oh, there you are, you bad boy!" she cooed to him in her baby voice. "I've been worried sick about you. Don't ever run off like that on me again. I've got to put that license on you."

Nick eyed them both in disgust. "You are way too attached to that thing."

"Shut up." She nuzzled his fur with her cheek and wondered what kind of mischief he'd been getting into. He smelled like fresh air and damp leaves. Holding him in her arms, she said, "That witch is going to try to take him from me. I can tell. I told her he was a dog, but she's not stupid. It's only a matter of time before she finds out."

Nick laughed. "You're taking a big risk. She'll have it taken away and slap you with a big fine. Or worse."

"I know. He won't even wear the license, so she has reason to take him. And I can't believe she's trying to tax me fifteen percent. That's going to sink my business, fast."

"Right. But don't get too rattled. The motion hasn't passed yet."

"But it might. And the worst thing about the language barrier is that I have no idea who is for or against it. So what do you think? What else did the others say? Were they for or against the tax, do you think?"

Mason frowned. "You want the truth?"

The second Audrey nodded, she wasn't sure if she did.

"The top nacho always gets the most cheese."

She gave him an annoyed look. "What does that mean?"

"It means she's on top there. People listen to what she says. And if a tax like this is gonna sink you? I'd be getting ready to hold my breath."

CHAPTER ELEVEN

Hold my breath? How am I supposed to do that? she thought again the next day.

With an hour to spare in her schedule, Audrey went on a little mission. As she walked down the street, she kept thinking about Mason's words to her. He really thought Mimi was going to win. It was so wrong, that witch, taxing people just for being good citizens. Penalizing people for helping animals.

She found the address the Canadian executive had given her and tracked down the factory in question, where the stray cats were staying. There was a faded sign on the wall outside that said, *Il Figlio DeMarco*, half-hidden by tendrils of ivy. As she and Nick looked for a way inside, a kitten darted across the street, onto a ledge, and through an opening in the boards crisscrossing the window.

Nick scampered to the opening and sat there, picking at his collar with his paw.

"Hey. For the last time, leave that alone!" she said, nudging him with her knee. "It's for your own good. I'll let you take it off when we get home."

He let out a broken whimper, trying to curry her sympathy.

The fox was definitely sly, because she had to admit it was working. He looked so cute and miserable, and her heart drooped.

Doing her best to ignore him, she peeled open the rotting wooden board and peered inside the vast room. The mostly brick building was full of dust, more rotting boards, and old machinery.

She went to slip inside, but before she could, Nick barreled inside, fearless.

Luckily, it was daylight, and there were several wide, frosted shop windows overhead, providing a bit of light, so Audrey was able to avoid all the obstacles in the way as she followed the fox deeper into the factory. He kept turning around, as if to say, *Hurry up! This way.* She stayed close by, weaving around the rusting old skeletons of what looked like industrial-sized textile looms and equipment with massive spools of tattered, colorless yarn.

She found her fox friend in a manager's office, complete with a wooden desk, chair, and filing cabinets, all feathery with dust. When she rounded the corner of the desk, she saw a pile of rags in the corner of the room, shaped into a little nest. On the rags, there was a new mother cat, along with six or seven rambunctious kittens, about two or three weeks old.

"Jackpot," Audrey said with a smile, kneeling down in front of them. The black striped mother cat climbed to her feet and sweetly approached her, bowing her head to her outstretched hand to be petted. By sight, though they were slightly unkempt, they looked fairly healthy. "Oh, aren't you sweet?"

She opened the cardboard carrying crate she'd brought and with Nick's surprisingly good shepherding skills, managed to get the entire family rounded up and into the carrier. Lifting it, she smiled through the holes at them. The mother poked her whiskered nose out, mewling softly, concerned and confused.

"Don't worry, Mama. I will take good care of you and your kiddos!"

I hope, at least, she thought as she carried the crate out to the curb. *If I can figure out how to pay for this gig.*

Last night, in bed with Nick at her side, she'd gone over the financials, trying to see what else she could squeeze from her budget if the fifteen percent tax did become a reality. It was bare bones as it was; there wasn't much to cut. The animals needed food, bedding, medicine, and other essentials. She could possibly hold a drive to collect those items from residents, but like Mimi had said, a lot of the residents of Mussomeli were poor, which meant donations probably wouldn't flow freely. Of course, with more expats moving in, buying homes, bringing in foreign money, that could change. But that could take months. Right now, she was in big trouble.

"Mimi Catalano," she muttered as she walked back to the clinic. Since she'd spent most of her adult life alone, she'd always had a habit of talking to the animals she cared for like they were people. Talking things out to them always made her feel better. "You have to stay away from her. She's not a friend of ours. Let's get you guys in and start taking care of you before I get taxed into oblivion, okay?"

When she arrived at the clinic, she set up an area for the new family in the cat area, away from the other pets, so that they could explore a little before she checked them out, and left out food and water.

"I'll have to give you all your check-ups later, when I get back. I have a lunch date! So be good!" she called, grabbing her purse.

This lunch date wasn't actually a date. She had to go to G's cafe. He'd texted her earlier that morning, telling her that his part-time dishwasher was a fifteen-year-old pet-lover who was looking to volunteer with animals a couple hours a week. Audrey said she'd love to meet him, so she arranged to stop there for lunch, but really… there was practically no way she would refuse the free help.

As she was locking up the clinic, her phone buzzed with a call from "UNKNOWN CALLER" with the number blocked. She answered it. "Hello?"

After a long pause, right as Audrey was about to hang up, a heavily accented voice said, *"Audrey Smart?"*

"Yes. Who is this?"

"There is… an animal… out here… a dog." The voice sounded strained, distant, and there was a loud noise in the background, as if the person was speaking in a wind tunnel.

Audrey gripped the phone closer to her ear. "I'm sorry. I can barely hear you. Out where?"

"At *Lago Sfendato*. Outside Mussomeli."

Audrey hadn't been in Sicily long enough to know many of the points of interest on the island, but *Lago Sfendato* was one she knew. She'd passed it a few days prior, on her drive to the coast with G. It was probably fifteen minutes outside of town, so not far.

But the bigger problem was, Audrey didn't have a car. She'd have to ask Mason to borrow his, and he'd probably throw a fit. The last thing she wanted to do was ask him for another favor. He'd carried on for days the last time she borrowed it.

At that moment, she didn't have a choice.

"Well, is it a stray? I can't get there right now, but if you bring him into my office tomorrow, I can—"

"It's injured. Please come. Now."

Injured? That made a difference. Audrey never could let any animal suffer.

She started to ask the caller for his name, but realized after a few moments of dead air that he'd hung up. "Hello?" she asked, receiving no response. "Hello?"

She pocketed her phone, went back inside, grabbed her travel medical bag, and rushed to Mason's place. His little powder blue Fiat was outside, but when she knocked on the door, he didn't answer. She knocked until her knuckles hurt, louder and louder, thinking of that poor, injured dog on the lakeside. Just as she was about to give up, the door opened a crack.

It was Mason, as she'd never seen him before… wearing nothing but tight-fitting boxer briefs. The man loved to show off his world-class abs unabashedly. But now, *everything* was hanging out. His longish cinnamon hair was a mess on his head, his blue eyes bleary. He yawned and leaned a defined bicep against the door jamb. "What are you doing here, Boston?"

Audrey had the typical reaction—her eyes bulged, and her cheeks steamed. She fought to collect herself. "Um ..." she giggled. "Were you sleeping? It's after eleven."

He stretched his arms over his head, flexing his muscles and hollowing out his abdomen in a way that was so mesmerizing, Audrey could've watched it all day. "Well, with that little wrench Catalano threw in my renovation plans, I don't really got much of an agenda, you know."

"Good. Then you won't be using your car? I need it."

He went from half-asleep to wide-awake in a split second. "Uh. No."

She'd expected push-back, but not outright refusal. "What? Why? You need to take your *guest* out to see the sights?"

He laughed. "My *guest*"—he used the same inflection she'd used—"doesn't arrive till next week. You do recall what you did the last time I let you use it? You nearly dropped the transmission in the middle of the road."

She rolled her eyes. She hadn't been that incompetent with the stick shift, but he was such a baby when it came to his car. "Come on. I wouldn't ask you unless I really needed it. There's an injured dog outside of town that needs my help."

"So you're planning to put a *dog* in my car? A drooling, pooping, shedding, disgusting beast that'll probably screw up my upholstery?" He shook his head. "That's not just a no, Boston. That's a hell no."

She clasped her hands together and stuck out her lower lip, begging. "Then I guess I'll just have to ask someone else!"

In answer, he slammed the door on her.

Great. She really hadn't expected the same tactic her animals used on her to work on him. Animals were far cuter. Well, there was still G. He'd be more than happy to lend her anything she wanted. Of course. She should've asked him first.

She took the first step off Mason's stoop when the door suddenly opened behind her and Mason appeared, tucking a T-shirt into his jeans and dangling his keychain from the other hand. He jogged over to the driver's side. "Get in. I'll drive."

Audrey crossed her arms. "It's fine. I wouldn't want to hurt your precious baby. I'll just ask G."

He slid into the car and glared at her through the passenger-side window. "Sit your butt in this car now, and lead the way."

"Fine," she said as if she was doing him a favor. She threw her bag in the back and flopped down in the seat as he donned mirrored, Top Gun sunglasses and started up the car. Loud country music filled the cabin as he shifted and headed down the narrow street. She gave him directions and he drummed his fingers casually on the wheel as he made his way out of the city.

"So now you're taking care of strays *outside* the city?" he observed as he turned down the radio. "What's the deal? I thought you didn't have the money or the—"

"I don't," she cut him off, because she didn't want to think about. "I don't even know where it is, but I got a call about an injured animal, and I'm not—"

"You have a big heart, girl. But you also got an empty head. You have a business to run. And you said it was hanging by a thread."

"It is. But I can't do nothing. There's an animal that needs me. And I don't abandon my responsibilities." *Like my father.* She pushed that thought away. She'd been doing fine the past few days not thinking about him, even though the renovation project was something he'd have excelled at. "This person called me for help, so it's up to me to respond."

"Person? Who was it?"

She shrugged. "I don't know. Someone. A man. Maybe a woman. They didn't leave a name."

He whipped off his sunglasses and stared at her. "Let me get this straight. You got called by an anonymous guy, and you thought it was a good idea to go out to the middle of nowhere to meet him, by yourself?"

"Um. Yeah."

"You got rocks for brains? You don't think that's a little dangerous? Little thing like you? What if it was a murderer?"

She laughed. "This is Mussomeli. It's very safe. I'm fine. I can take care of myself."

He eyed her doubtfully. To be honest, she wasn't sure either. It was pure luck that she'd been able to get out of her scrape with the lumber supplier who'd murdered the foreman. If it hadn't been for Nick interceding at just the right time, she might not have escaped with her life.

But really, what did he want to do? Be her bodyguard? Sometimes she just didn't get him. Overly concerned, almost possessive one moment, completely aloof the next. She couldn't fight the feeling that he was playing games with her, just to make her dangle on a chain like the rest of his many admirers.

When they reached the sign for the lake, she instructed him to pull off on the side of the road and then unclipped her seatbelt. As she opened the door, he said, "Do you know where you're going?"

"No," she said, scanning the area. A long line of blue, which must've been the lake, stretched in the distance, occasionally visible beyond the trees. "Whoever called was not very specific. I guess I'll just walk around."

He scrambled to pull off his seatbelt and follow after her. "How do you know it's not just a crank? Sounds like a crank."

"I don't. But I'm going to check it out. Just in case."

The lake was set back far from the road, down a fairly steep incline through a forest. Audrey took the path, sliding in her sneakers on the loose dirt. A couple of times, she had to reach out to steady herself, and the only thing there to grab ahold of was Mason's ridiculously hard chest. Every time she did so, she blushed a little more, until he finally took her elbow and helped her down, letting out a chuckle. "Sure, you can take care of yourself."

She snatched her arm away. "I'm fine," she snapped. The pathway was evening out anyway, putting her on more solid ground.

A five-minute walk down a narrow, tree-lined grove, and they emptied out onto a rocky beach. She held a hand over her eyes to shield them from the sun as she scanned the place. There were a few houses, spaced far apart among the trees, beyond a wooden fence. The sand was smooth, as if no one had been there in a while, and as far as she could see in both directions, deserted. "Wow. I didn't realize it was so big."

"So you're just gonna walk around this lake, looking for an injured dog?"

That had been her plan. But now she realized even just walking the perimeter of the lake might take her until well after dusk. She heaved a breath and started walking. "What else can I do? I have to try."

She moved purposefully through the sand to the edge of the lake. The water was mirror-calm, with small waves lapping at the stony shore. The sun from a cloudless sky dappled thousands of diamonds on the surface. It really was beautiful. In America, this place would've been swamped with beachgoers, soaking up the sun on this perfect day. But this area of Sicily was empty and desolate.

Eventually, she came to a place where she noticed footprints in the sand. Many footprints. Though no one was around at this hour, it appeared to be a popular spot.

Not caring if Mason was following, she left the wide expanse of beach and walked beyond a rock ledge that had been carved out by the lake. It was about chest-high, effectively sealing her away from view of anyone on the beach. As she went around a bend, she saw a large creature racing toward her. In the distance, it looked like a small horse.

But as it got closer, she realized it was a giant gray mastiff.

The only thing was, it didn't look injured at all.

Barking excitedly, it jumped up on her, the force of the collision nearly toppling her to the ground. She grabbed ahold of its front legs before it could knock her over, and its massive body towered over her. It moved its muzzle toward her to lick her face. "Oh!" she laughed, checking for a collar. "Okay, cutie! I know you're excited."

No collar. So he was a stray? She looked up the beach for the owner, but the white sands stretched into the distance, completely empty.

Mason caught up with her. "What is th—" He let out a groan as the animal started to attack him with kisses, too. He shoved it off of him. "Get. Off. Geesh. What the hell is that? A mutant? That damn thing ain't goin' in my car. Ain't even gonna fit in there."

Without warning, it let out a sharp bark and bounded back in the direction it came from. When it got a few steps away, it stopped and turned, waiting for them.

"He doesn't have a collar. I think he wants us to follow him," Audrey said. "Don't you want us to follow you, boy?"

"Why are you talking to it like that?"

"Like what?"

"Like it's your pride and freaking joy. It's a horse that nearly maimed you."

"I always—"

He wiped his hand on his jeans. "Holy—what's wrong with it? That thing is like a drool machine."

She nudged his shoulder. "Mason. Focus. The dog's trying to tell us something."

"*Not* goin' in my car, you hear?"

She smacked him. "Come on. He might lead us to the injured dog."

She broke into a run, with Mason on her heels. That didn't last long. Audrey never had been one for exercise, so he quickly overtook her and widened the lead as she panted, getting a stabbing stitch in her side. Meanwhile, Mason strode ahead like he'd been born running ultramarathons. After they rounded a bend and came to another beach, she called out, breathless, "Wait. Hold on."

He turned, hardly out of breath, as she nearly collapsed. She doubled over, sucking the air into her lungs. Holding out a finger, she wheezed, "One second. I'm dying."

Mason eyed her pitifully. "You're serious? You should go running with that girl… what's her name? The one across the street from you. The hot girl."

"I'd rather boil my head in a lobster pot, thanks," she muttered.

He shrugged. "Just sayin'. Could do you some good."

"The vapid conversation alone would kill me."

The dog had stopped, too, on the other side of the beach, and was now looking back at them, barking and pounding the sand with its massive paws, urging them forward.

Lungs still on fire, she broke into a run, but within a few paces, Mason quickly sprang ahead of her. The dog didn't go any farther, though. He stayed at the edge of the beach, and when she got close enough, she noticed a large black heap at his feet.

The injured dog, likely.

She sped up just as Mason came to an abrupt halt, so fast that she nearly slammed into his back.

"What—" she began, but the rest of the words died in her throat as she followed his line of sight to the injured animal.

Because it wasn't an injured dog lying in the sand at all.

It was a person. A woman, lying face-down on the sand. From the position she was in, one might have thought she was only sunbathing, except everything else about her was all wrong. She was wearing a red jogging suit, the sleeve of the jacket torn, and one of her heels was missing. The visible part of her skin, just a cheek, really, half-hidden by her wild black hair, was a ghostly pale.

"Oh my god," she whispered, as she caught sight of the red hair clip, hopelessly lost among her black, crazy curls. There was something else in her hair, right over her ear, something viscous, matted with sand. Blood. Audrey's stomach lurched. "Is she …"

"I don't know." Mason crouched over her, pushed her hair aside, and felt her neck for a pulse. "Yeah. I think so. But you're the doctor."

Right, she was. But she made no movement to confirm his suspicion. There was a reason she'd gone into veterinary medicine and not human medicine… the cuteness of the animals made up for the unpleasantness of some things. Things like death. And she was staunchly against euthanasia because she hated the idea of any living being dying before its time.

"Wait… is that …"

A strong sense of déjà vu gripped Audrey, making her knees wobble. Before, she'd been gasping for air, but now she forgot how to breathe.

She knew this woman.

It was the councilwoman herself, Mimi Catalano.

CHAPTER TWELVE

Audrey sat on a rock at the edge of the lake, on the other side of the beach from the crime scene where a dozen members of *la polizia* gathered. Shivering, she wiped the rest of the tears from her eyes and stared out across the lake, lazily petting the mastiff, who huddled by her side.

Two.

She'd found two bodies in the two months she'd been in Mussomeli. Wasn't that weird? She certainly hadn't gotten desensitized to it… finding Mimi Catalano lying there wasn't any less shocking than the first dead body she'd found. She shuddered at the thought of the bloody wound, matted with hair and sand.

"Hey."

She looked up to find Mason standing there, hands in his pockets. He'd been talking to the police, telling them everything they needed to know about the grisly discovery.

He lowered himself onto the rock next to her. "You okay?"

"I've been better."

"Yeah. I'll bet. The police want to talk to you. You ready?"

Right. They had to interview them separately, so they'd corroborate each other's story. She nodded and slid off the rock. She knew this drill. It was only a matter of time before they cornered her to get her side of it. "Yeah. Where?"

He surveyed the group of officers and pointed to a man in a blazer and khakis, who was crouching in the sand, head tilted awkwardly to the side as he picked up something in the sand with a pair of forceps. "That one."

Audrey knew him. It was Detective DiNardo.

Thank goodness for small favors, she thought as she trudged through the sand toward him. DiNardo had led the investigation on the case of the foreman. Originally, he'd suspected Audrey, as had most of the town, but when the real killer was caught, he'd eaten crow. She'd looked after his kitten's conjunctivitis, too, so he liked her. This wouldn't take long.

"Hello, Detective," she said when he looked up.

"Well, if it isn't the American veterinarian," he said with a smile. "Trouble seems to follow you around, doesn't it?"

Audrey shrugged. "I wish it didn't, but it appears so."

"Mussomeli's had five murders in the past five years," he said, holding out a hand, fingers splayed. "And you've found two of them. What do you have to say about that?"

Audrey sighed. "I'd say that makes me really unlucky." *But I'm not entirely surprised.*

DiNardo walked toward the line of scrubby bushes surrounding the beach, studying a small notebook in his hands. "So, Audrey, your boyfriend says you two found the body while you were walking this beach? At what time was this?"

"He's not my boyfriend," she quickly corrected. *Wait, did Mason say that he was?* "And we weren't going on a walk for exercise. But yes, we did. At around twelve-thirty."

"You said it wasn't for exercise. What led you out this way?"

"I got a call. An anonymous one. From someone… here." She fished her phone out of her pocket and navigated to the incoming calls. There was one marked UNKNOWN CALLER. She showed it to him. "The person asked for me and told me that there was an injured dog out here. So since I don't have a car, I asked to borrow my neighbor's, Mason's, and he drove me. While we were looking for the dog, we found her, like that."

"This call… did you recognize the voice?"

"No. It was hard to hear. But I think it was a man. His voice sounded deep. Kind of agitated."

He nodded and wrote something down. "Did you know the victim?"

Audrey nodded. "I did. I—" She stopped when she realized *I was in a big public confrontation with her at a council meeting last night* probably would incriminate her. But then again, there were a hundred people at that meeting. It would likely come out. "I saw her last night. At a council meeting. She was proposing a tax on people who take in strays that would threaten my livelihood. So I was there to speak out against it."

He looked up from his pad, eyes narrowed. "Is that so?"

She rolled her eyes. "Yes. I get it, that gives me a motive. But I don't have means."

"Sure you do. Rock. Back of head. Anyone could've done it."

"Yeah, but Mason was with me. He can tell you—"

"He told me that the victim shut down his renovation project and is causing him a lot of costly changes."

She stared at him. "So, what are you suggesting? That the two of us conspired to kill her?"

Audrey almost laughed at the idea. She and Mason fought about everything. Yes, they may have been united in their hate for the woman, but that was where their agreement ended. He'd want to strangle Mimi, and she'd want to poison her. It'd never work. They'd be like the Laurel and Hardy of criminals.

But DiNardo didn't laugh. He simply shrugged. "We don't have an exact time of death either. It could've happened earlier in the day. Could you tell me your movements today?"

"My movements? I don't know. I was at work until about ten. I saw a couple appointments. And then I went to an old factory on the south side of town to collect some strays I'd gotten a complaint about," she said, thinking, *Great, no one saw me get those strays. I don't have an alibi.* "After that, I was going to meet a friend, but then I got the call and I came right here."

"I see." He wrote this down.

Why, when he looked at her, did she get the feeling he doubted every word she was saying? "I don't have a car, so it'd be pretty impossible for me to get here on my own," she pointed out.

"Hmmm," he said, looking up the beach. "The other officers say there's a path from the city somewhere. I need to check it out."

She looked up. From here, the city proper rose out into the hillside, not all that far away. At least, not far away enough to exonerate her from the suspect list. *Of course there is.*

"I didn't know about that path."

He wrote something on his pad. "Mmmhmm."

"She was wearing a jogging suit. Maybe she was just here to get some exercise, and a random robber attacked her?" Audrey suggested.

"Exercising in the sand, wearing heels?" He shook his head. "From what I hear, she wore jogging outfits everywhere. Besides, she had a lot of cash on her. A diamond wedding ring. Nothing was taken."

"Oh. Huh. So you think someone lured her out here, so they'd be alone, and killed her? For what?"

"We'll figure it out." He reached into his blazer and pulled out a plastic bag. In the plastic bag was a large, fist-sized hunk of rock, sharp on one end. When he held it up, Audrey noticed that one end of it was stained in brownish red. "This here appears to be the weapon. It's one of the rocks from the beach, likely. And with something like this, a woman could've killed her, just as easily as a man."

Her stomach somersaulted. "I'm sure. But the fact is that I didn't do it."

"All right," the detective said. "I'm not saying you did. And no, you're not under arrest. But still, for the investigation …"

"I know, I know," Audrey said. "Don't leave town. Been there, done that."

That was okay. She had plenty to focus on at work, anyway. She peered down the beach at the mastiff, who was following Mason, though Mason seemed to want nothing to do with it. What had that dog seen? Maybe he'd seen the whole grisly event.

Deep in thought, she started to walk away, when DiNardo said, "And Audrey?"

She turned.

"Don't …" He paused, as if he was trying to find the right words. "Don't do anything stupid."

"Me? Of course I won't."

But Audrey knew what he was referring to. She couldn't help being curious where mysteries were concerned. The last idea she'd had, she wound up tracking down the culprit… but it could have been very different. It could have gotten her killed.

It wasn't wise to take chances and push what little luck she had.

CHAPTER THIRTEEN

"I'm a sucker," Mason muttered under his breath as he drove Audrey back into town.

"What do you mean?" Audrey said, leaning over to turn down the terrible country-rock twang that had been blasting out of the speakers. Even with the windows down, Mason liked to listen to the music so loud, her eardrums throbbed along with the music.

He let out a bitter laugh but didn't answer.

It was only when she leaned forward to play with the dial that she got a glimpse of him, because there was a giant, panting wall of dog sitting between them. And yes, he was drooling mightily onto the center console, big globs of it, some of which splashed upon their bare elbows whenever the wind blew just so. But he was so darn cute. Calm, but excited to be in their company. A big, well-behaved sweetheart of an animal.

"What do you mean? Him?" She pointed at the mastiff, then rubbed his sad, soft jowls. She lowered her hand and he gave her his paw. "Stop. Look at that! He's trained. He's such a good little dog."

"Little?"

"Whatever." Audrey just didn't get Mason. First, he had no heart. Second, how could he be fixated on such a small thing, like this wondrously beautiful animal, ruining his car, when there was an actual murderer running around? "I can't believe that happened. Can you believe it? Mimi Catalano. Geesh. How can you be so calm about it?"

"I don't know. Why aren't you calmer? This is your second one. Thought you'd be a pro by now."

"Ha ha. That one was an accident. This one wasn't. She was targeted. Doesn't that freak you out?"

"Not really. Besides, how do you know she was targeted?"

"Well, obviously, she had a lot of enemies. And she crossed the wrong one." She sighed. Other than his own reflection, the guy wasn't one to get excited about anything. "You're weird."

"No, think about it. I'd be more freaked if it was random. I moved halfway across the world for a certain way of life. And that way of life didn't include muggings and killings and street crimes I could've found in downtown Charleston." He shrugged. "You know, our property values'll go way down if this becomes a habit."

"You're *so* weird. If it becomes a habit, I think we'll have more to worry about than whether we can sell our homes," she muttered. "We'll probably be hiding in our closets, trying to evade this cunning serial murderer who has been evading police all around this small town. Anyway, that doesn't happen outside of America. Serial killing is a distinctly American phenomenon."

"Says who?"

"Everyone. Look it up."

"No. I don't need to. Hello… Jack the Ripper?"

"Oh, whatever. Doesn't matter. This person was clearly insane. It's scary to think someone planned to murder someone. Normal people don't actually think that way. Who do you think did it?"

He shrugged. "Like you said, not counting either of us, the woman had a lot of enemies. It wasn't like she was beloved by all. I'm surprised we're not hearing the chorus of 'Ding, dong, the witch is dead' from out here."

"That doesn't really narrow it down at all, does it?" she said, thinking. "Really. About half that room last night hated her guts."

"The other half was probably just lying about not hating them. And there are about that many people who are better off now that she's gone. Like you."

"And you, too," she pointed out.

He chuckled as he upshifted. "Yeah, but when I said I wanted to wring the witch's neck, I meant it in the figurative sense. Besides, I'm not the insane, murdering type."

She raised an eyebrow. "Oh. Right. You're just too good-looking."

He nodded matter-of-factly. "Make love, not war."

Just then, the dog leaned his drooly chin on Audrey's shoulder. She peered into his big sad eyes and rubbed his wet muzzle. "Oh, baby. We're almost there. Don't worry."

Mason downshifted as they passed the Mussomeli city limits sign, and the asphalt streets became cobblestone once again. The facades of the ancient baroque architecture, golden in the sinking sun, and the brightly painted shutters were a welcome sight after what they'd seen. He mumbled, "I love it when you call me baby."

"I was talking to the dog."

"I know. No accounting for taste. You got me here, and instead you're drooling over that ugly dog the way he drools all over my car. Gross."

She let out a groan of disapproval. Mason was so used to being adored, he simply hated when attention wasn't on him. How could anyone hate this creature? The dog was quiet, attentive, and well-mannered, and he just wanted love. It was clear he had an owner. *Someone* had trained him well. "I'm sorry, did you forget what just happened? We found a dead body. Stop being inappropriate."

"Me? Not appropriate?" He scoffed, feigning shock. "Never."

"*Always.*" She shuddered again at the thought of Mimi, lying on that cold beach. Wanting to fill her mind with something else, she cycled back to the nicest thing she'd seen that morning, and winced. "I mean, really. Answering the door this morning, half-naked? What are you trying to do, give people heart attacks?"

"Just you." He flashed her that dimpled smirk. "You deserve it. You're the one who interrupted my beauty sleep. Plus, you enjoyed the show. Admit it."

She snorted to hide the fact that she was blushing again at the thought. Thank goodness they were turning onto *Via Barcellona.* "Drop us off at my clinic. I'm late for my two o'clock appointment. And I need to check on Polpetto here."

"Polpetto?"

"It means 'Meatball.' I googled it."

"Great." He pulled to the curb. "And to think I actually used to like meatballs."

"Stop. You love him."

Polpetto clumsily jumped out with her, then sat on the curb like a good boy. He didn't even need to be leashed. Definitely a good boy. Some dog owners paid big bucks for that kind of training.

She leaned into the car's window. "Maybe you can do me a favor?"

He dipped his sunglasses. "Sexual?"

She couldn't help it. Her cheeks flamed and she let out a giggle. "Really. Stop being gross. Have some respect for the dead."

"But it's so fun." He winked, then turned serious. "All right. What?"

"He's a big dog. One you really can't miss. Someone has to know who owned him. So if you wouldn't mind... keep an ear open? If you hear of anyone who's missing a dog, or see anyone suspicious ..."

He nodded. "You'll be the first to know."

"Thanks. And thanks for the ride."

He shifted the car into drive. "Always an adventure with you, Boston."

As he drove off, she looked down at the giant mastiff, who was waiting patiently for her.

Nick suddenly arrived on the curb and started hissing at him. Though the fox was clearly outsized, he stood his ground, getting into attack mode.

Polpetto just stared at his opponent like, *I'm not going to get into this with you.*

"Easy, Nick," Audrey said to him. "You're always number one in my heart. But this guy needs a place to stay at the Hotel Smart. Let's make him welcome."

Again, she gave the stray dog her hand, and he put his own in it, to shake. *Yes, you are a very good dog. Someone must be missing you. I wonder if we can find out who that person is, because maybe they were on that beach, too. And maybe they have a story to tell...*

"Come on, baby," she whispered to him. "Let's go get you a nice collar."

*

By the time Audrey finished with her afternoon appointments and taking care of the new batch of strays in the clinic, it was after six in the evening. She said goodbye to Polpetto and the other animals, then locked up and went to La Mela Verde. When she stepped inside, the café was standing room only, buzzing with the dinner crowd.

She saw G, working so hard with the evening rush that he didn't even look her way. A beautiful woman with bright red hair was waiting the tables, someone Audrey had never seen before. Was that Valentina? She had to wonder as she found an open seat in the corner of the bar and as she slipped onto the stool. She could see the two of them together, as a couple.

Suddenly, a voice said, "Well, if it isn't the lady of the hour. You've been busy today, huh?"

Audrey groaned inwardly as she lifted a menu, wishing she could shield herself from view. She knew that voice, but she'd never heard it here at the café, her refuge. She spun on the stool to see Nessa sitting at a table with a couple of handsome, suited men, a salad and glass of wine in front of her.

"Nessa," she muttered. "Hello."

"Hi!" Nessa said. "This is Frederic, my agent, and Boone, my producer. We were just going over details of my HGTV show, and we were talking about interesting neighbors that I might have to include, to add some color to our episode. Of course, most of it's going to be focused on me, but I mentioned you might make an amusing couple minutes of airtime."

Audrey stiffened. Around her, people seemed to be taking notice, paying attention, likely because Nessa's voice was ten times louder than the regular chatter. Audrey's only thought was to get Nessa off her back as soon as possible. "Thanks, but I don't think so."

"Why not? You're like Mussomeli's own Grim Reaper. Wherever you go, death follows," she said, lifting her glass of wine to her lips and smiling.

Audrey winced. Did she...? No. She couldn't. Not this soon. They'd only discovered Mimi Catalano lying dead on the beach this afternoon.

"So is it true that you found the body of that councilwoman today? It's all over the news around here."

Audrey had moved to Sicily, at least partially because she thought the slower pace of things would do her good. Apparently, news traveled even faster here than in the States. This was like a world record. "It's on the news?"

She nodded. "Oh, yes. Of course. People can't stop talking about it. So didn't the police think it odd that you were the one who discovered both bodies? I mean, that can't be a coincidence. First, just innocently stumbling on a dead man in my backyard when you had no business being there, and then stumbling upon another one on a deserted beach? Odd!"

"I—"

"And wait. That councilwoman. Wasn't she the one reaming you out the other day because of some missing permits?" She tilted her head inquisitively. "So you knew her. Curiouser and curiouser."

Audrey's lips twisted. "I got an anonymous call about an injured dog. It led me out there. And I wasn't alone. I was with Mason."

She blinked her little doe eyes. "Anonymous phone call? Yeah, right. Oh, Mason, hmmm? Is that the American contractor?" She leaned over to the men and said, "He's the one I told you *definitely* needs to be in the series. Give the American housewives some beefcake to drool over. They'll thank me, big time."

The men nodded obediently, and the one in horn-rimmed glasses typed something into the small laptop near his butter dish. Men always listened extra hard when Nessa spoke.

"So are you saying you were framed?" she asked Audrey. "Who would frame you?"

Audrey blinked. She hadn't thought of it that way, but yes. That's what it looked like. Who would've done that? She hadn't lived here long enough to have enemies. At least, she didn't think so. Well, except Nessa.

"Principessa!"

Thank goodness for the distraction. She turned on her stool, but as she did, the man and the woman on either side of her vacated their stools almost in unison. What, did she have cooties? She looked around and realized several other people in the restaurant were glaring at her, but they looked away the moment she made eye contact.

Great. Nessa had nearly made her a pariah before, upon the murder of the foreman. Audrey had barely had a chance to get over the stigma, and now it felt like it was slipping over her again. Maybe they all did think she was the Grim Reaper of Mussomeli.

"What can I get you, *cara*?" he said, touching her hand flirtatiously. "Missed you for lunch."

Audrey hadn't been planning on drinking when she came in, but now she wanted to order a long and tall of whatever would take the edge off quicker. "Whatever it is, make it a double. It's been a day. Sorry I wasn't able to come over for lunch. I really wanted to meet that boy you had in mind for the volunteering."

"It's okay," G said with a warm smile. His eyes shifted over to where Nessa sat, and he shook his head. "Sounds like you've been busy. The boy isn't here now—he only works lunch. But I'll send him over to you tomorrow. Early in the morning. Okay?"

"Yes." She sighed with relief. "Thank you. I really need the help."

"He's a good boy. Worked for me two years. You like." He poured her a glass of red wine. "Here. On the house, as you say!"

"Thank you." She brought it to her lips and took a sip that turned into a gulp, swallowing the bitter taste down, hoping to calm her nerves.

"Ah, Dottore Smart!" a voice called behind her.

She whirled again to see Orlando Falco standing in the doorway, a worried expression marring his handsome features, his normally slicked back white hair tumbling over his brow. He headed over to her, navigating around the tightly packed tables.

"I've been looking all over for you," he said, resting an arm on the bar. He nodded at G. "Hello, G. How's business?"

G waved and set out another glass, pouring it for the councilman. "As you can tell. Pretty good."

"I guess you've heard about Mimi," Audrey said, polishing off her glass of wine in record speed. It helped a little, but her nerves were still shot.

"Yes. Regrettable. And such a shock. I heard you found the body."

Audrey nodded. How did he know that? With a grapevine like this town's, who needed the media? "Yes. It's terrible."

He let out a laugh tinged with sadness. "To be honest, I know a lot of people won't be missing her that much. But it does worry me. For you."

"For me?"

"Yes. It's no secret that you had no love for her ..." he said, looking at his glass. "And I worry ..."

For a politician, he was uncharacteristically awkward with whatever he was trying to say. But she understood. She saw it in the faces of the people around her, watching her. "I get it. Even just being suspected of murder probably wouldn't be very good for my business?"

He nodded. "Regrettably."

"I understand. But I didn't kill her. I just found the body."

"Yes, I know. Of course. But that doesn't mean people won't talk." People like Nessa. Especially Nessa. "A stranger, new to town, who had a very public spat with the victim? Not only that, Ms. Catalano had a lot of supporters on the board, pushing for that tax, so it's still very much alive. If it does go through, not only will you have to contend with the tax, but I fear, after this, no one will want to adopt the strays you've taken in."

"I understand," she said, motioning to G to refill her glass. "I don't plan on backing down on the tax, whoever I have to fight. And if I have to prove myself innocent of murder in the process, *again*, then I will."

"All right." He patted her hand. "I just wanted to let you know."

As he turned to leave, Audrey looked over her shoulder. Nessa was now talking to the waitress, and the two of them were staring right at her. The waitress looked terrified, as if she was staring into the eyes of the devil herself.

This is nothing new, Audrey thought.

But now she had so much more on her plate. She had to think about the lives of the animals in Mussomeli, too. They depended on her. How could she do that, and clear her name, at the same time?

CHAPTER FOURTEEN

The next day, when someone knocked on her door, Audrey plastered a bright, welcoming smile on her face as she opened it, expecting the awkward Sicilian teenager that G had promised to send her way. She *had* to make this work.

When she saw Mason standing there, she sighed in disappointment. "Oh. It's just you." She left the door open and trudged to the coffee maker, where she'd just poured herself an espresso.

He lingered in the doorway for a second before coming in. "I think that's the warmest welcome I've ever received, Boston."

She snorted. Likely, his arrival at places was met with great fanfare—confetti and cheers and balloons. Especially where women were present. "Sorry. I was waiting for someone. I had an eight o'clock appointment."

Nick tried to cuddle up to his ankles. Mason extricated himself and gave the fox *Stay away* eye daggers before checking his phone. "It's eight-thirty."

"I know. Ugh." She slumped into her chair and took a too-big sip of the hot espresso, scalding her tongue. "He's not showing. And I really needed him."

He leaned against the door jamb and said, casually, "Hot date?"

Was that jealousy? No, not with Mason. Probably a joke, considering people rarely dated at eight in the morning. "A teenager. He was going to volunteer at the clinic. You know, taking appointments and answering the phone, caring for the animals, stuff like that." She stood up, looking frantically for her bag as she thought of her massive to-do list. "I can't stay here. I've got to get to the clinic."

He started to back out as she realized something.

"Wait. What are you doing here? It's early for you, isn't it?"

He nodded. "On the way to the hardware store. I'm thinking without that Catalano woman to hold my feet to the flame, I can finally get some work done."

"Oh. That's nice." He was still standing in the doorway, in her way. "Excuse me."

He hesitated there just long enough for her to be curious.

"Was there something else you wanted?"

He shrugged. "Just checking on you. Making sure you're okay, after yesterday."

"I'm fine. I mean, I have enough on my plate. I could probably do without people accusing me of another murder," she muttered, peering past him, out the door. "I mean, that's probably why this kid never showed up. People look at me like I'm a felon. And thanks to Nessa, who has some sort of death wish for me, people actually think I'm responsible for it. Even if I'd wanted to murder someone... like I have the time?"

She threw her hands up, forgetting she had her coffee mug in one of them. It dribbled over the side, scalding her hand. She let out a scream and a curse, set the coffee down, and went to run it under the cold tap.

"Whoa. You don't look fine. You're stressed."

Really? Thank you, Sherlock. She shut off the faucet and, lacking any nearby towel, shook her hand maniacally in front of her. "It's not just the murder. It's everything. It's always times like this that I want to pack things in and go home. But once again, I can't, because DiNardo says I can't leave the city."

"Nah. You can't go home. Look at everything you've accomplished so far."

She frowned. Of course, he was right. Starting her own clinic had been her dream, and now it was coming true. So what if it was a little rocky? She was almost there. She couldn't give that up now, even if she wanted to.

She picked up her coffee and, not having learned her lesson the first time, brought it to her lips and scalded them. She winced. "Well, fine. But not being on a suspect list would probably ease my worries significantly."

"I get it."

She eyed him doubtfully. He'd been there, same as her, and yet no one seemed to think he was the culprit. It was those little-boy dimples. Made him look innocent. Capable of no wrong. "Really, though. Can they believe they actually think I went all the way there, murdered her, and then came back to get you? I'd have absolutely no way of getting down there."

"I looked it up on the map. It's fifteen minutes by car, but there's a jogging path that connects the lake to Mussomeli. It's probably only ten minutes, on foot, if you're running."

Right. DiNardo had mentioned a path. "Oh. That makes me feel so much better." Her lips twisted. "Besides. You know how I run."

"Okay, a half hour, for you." He yawned. "But you see their point. According to the police, anyone from town could've been watching her, seen her heading out there, followed her down the path, and bonk."

Great. So that meant that because she was alone for a few hours prior to driving out there, which was more than enough time to get to the lake and back, she didn't have a solid alibi. "You don't have an alibi either. Unless the police want to question your pillow. You know what it is? It's Nessa. That's the reason why all this focus is on me. She loves spreading any dirt she can about me."

"Eh," he said, dismissing it. That was the problem. Hot people got let off the hook *way* too easy. "What I want to know is who called you?"

She pulled out her phone and looked at the incoming call log. "I don't know. I told the police about it, but the number was blocked. I keep mentally dissecting the call, trying to think if there's something I missed. But yes, it is interesting. Whoever did that is likely the killer, right?"

"Yes. So it reasons that if they knew about your beef with Catalano, they thought that by calling you there, they could frame you. You have enemies?"

She considered that for a moment. "Not really. Who would hate me? Well, other than Nessa. And everyone knew about my beef with Mimi Catalano. You know how many people were at that meeting."

He leaned against the door, thinking. "What did this call sound like?"

"I don't know. It was a man. Or maybe a woman. I couldn't tell. I think they were pretending to have an accent, you know?" She shrugged. "At times it sounded almost like an American, pretending to be foreign."

"I think that's what you go on."

She went to the door, finally succeeding in nudging him out of the way. "I can't *go on* anything. I have far too much to do now. Including getting a bunch of animals exercised and fed before I start with my full day of appointments—"

"I don't mean you specifically. I meant the police. You told them that, right? They need to look into it. You should stay out of it."

"I did tell them." At least, she thought she did. She couldn't remember. She shoved past him and grabbed the door, pulling it closed and locking it.

He was silent for a moment, pensive, which was totally unlike him. Before she could take a step off the front stoop, he said, "Okay, okay. You talked me into it."

She froze in place. "Into what?"

He started to walk her toward the clinic. "Helping you. I can probably wait a couple days before I get back to work on my reno."

Audrey forgot how to walk. She just stood there, waiting for the punch line. He might as well have told her he had a spare kidney to loan her. "What about your special, mysterious *guest*?"

"I got the dates mixed up. Turns out, she's not coming for another two weeks. I have time."

So it was a *she*. This was a big development in the whole Mystery of Mason's Guest saga, and yet she was too stupefied by his offer to appropriately acknowledge it. "Um… you do realize you'll be working with animals? The animals you hate?"

"I do. But I'll get over it." He continued to walk, hands in the pockets of his jeans, like he hadn't a care in the world. "Look. I'm a quick study, and I can't be sitting around with my thumb up my butt. I hate that. So do you want the help or not?"

Audrey rushed to catch up to him. Beggars couldn't be choosers. "Y-yes. Of course. You could fill in until I find someone suitable. That would be great."

"Good. So let's get over there, and you can show me what to do."

CHAPTER FIFTEEN

"Get the hell off me!"

No sooner had Audrey finished with her last patient of the day than she heard Mason screaming from the back of the clinic.

He'd been good, for the most part, and they'd passed an uneventful day, even though he'd been full of rather silly questions ("Do the cats eat the same thing as the dogs?") and had been more interested in charming people on the phone rather than taking care of the animals. But he'd filled their water and food dishes fine, even though he hadn't been one to cuddle or sweet-talk them while he did it.

That appeared to be backfiring on him, though. Animals could sense fear, and usually, they gravitated to it.

Which was completely evident when she ran into the back and found Mason lying flat on his stomach, Polpetto using him as a dog bed.

"Oh my gosh!" she shouted, rushing toward him. "Polpetto! Off!"

Polpetto listened, jumping off Mason at once and heeling beside her. Red-faced, clothes rumpled, Mason rolled over and stared at the ceiling. "What in God's name was that thing doing? I spilled some kibble and just bent down to pick it up, and that thing jumped on my back."

"That *thing* has a name. Polpetto." She stroked his ears as he stared up at her adoringly. "And he just wanted to play. He probably thought you wanted to wrestle. He needs his exercise. Whoever his owner was he's probably used to taking long walks with him."

He sat up and rested his forearms on his knees. "You can count me out for that one."

Mason had actually been a big help, so she couldn't ask for any more. Especially from an animal hater. She grabbed a leash and clipped it to Polpetto's collar. "Thanks. I'll take it from here."

They went out to the front, Mason massaging his lower back with both hands and eyeing Polpetto warily, the baby. "I can't believe it. How'd you get that thing wrapped around your finger?"

"What do you mean?"

"I mean, it listens to you. It's nice to you." He was staring at it as if trying to solve a particularly difficult math equation.

She laughed. "Well, I don't call it 'it' or 'that thing,' for starters! And I give it a little bit of love. Pets, cuddles, sweet talk. That's all you really need. And you'll get it back a thousandfold in return. That's what's so amazing about pets."

"Yeah. I'd rather get my love elsewhere. Thanks." He tried pulling his T-shirt around so he could see the back of it, and all Audrey glimpsed was a sliver of his tanned, glorious abs. She looked away as he whined, "Ugh. It drooled on my shirt. Look at that."

Don't look, Audrey. Don't look. "Aw, poor baby."

"See you tomorrow?"

She raised an eyebrow. "You're seriously coming back?"

"I said I would. I don't go back on my promises. Eight-thirty?"

She nodded. "Yes. Thanks." He turned to leave, and she stooped next to Polpetto. "And Mason?"

He whirled. "Yeah?"

Audrey cupped the mastiff's big jowls. "Polpetto says he's sorry. How can you resist this cute face?"

Mason was less than amused. "Try me." He let out a chuckle and turned back on his way. "'Night, Boston."

She smiled as she watched him leave, trying not to pay attention to how good his butt looked in those jeans. That was what he'd accused her of the first time she met him. People looked at Mason's *everything*, because it was all pretty exquisite. And yes, because of that, he was full of himself. But who knew that underneath, he was also a really nice guy?

No. The last thing she needed to do was think about him that way. He had a female guest coming to visit in two weeks. Probably a supermodel who was just as flawless as he was.

She stepped up the sidewalk, giving Polpetto the okay to start the walk, and the second she did, he took off, nearly pulling her arm out of its socket. No, she didn't like to run, but she didn't have much of a choice. During his check-up, she'd put Polpetto at a young three years, but he bounded up the street like a rambunctious puppy.

All she could do was hold on for dear life and hope he didn't pull her into the path of an oncoming car.

He led her around the town without stopping, almost as if he knew the streets well. Audrey didn't. She knew the path from the clinic to her house, and the few blocks around her home, pretty well, but the rest of the city was a mystery. He pulled her down back alleys and into private yards, rushing as if his life depended on it.

There were parts of the city she'd never seen before. Baroque-style churches. Quaint little tea and book shops. Statues and ancient ruins etched with time-worn symbols. Fenced-in olive trees on the sides of the street, hanging in a canopy overhead. Small, stone bridges over burbling creeks. Large, Greek-columned edifices mixed in between the small, sandwiched homes that must've been official buildings.

She saw none of this, really. Only as a blur, with a promise to come back later.

Finally, he stopped in a narrow alley that smelled of garbage. He sniffed at a couple of garbage cans.

"Oh, no you don't," she scolded him, massaging her sore shoulder. "You had dinner. This food isn't going to do you any favors."

"Principessa?"

She looked up to see G striding toward her, a heavy bag of garbage in each hand. Behind him, an open door spilled light into the dark alley. She looked up at the building. It had looked rather familiar, but she'd never seen La Mela Verde from the back. Polpetto had taken her up and down so many streets, she'd completely lost her sense of direction.

"What are you doing out here?" he asked, smiling down at the dog. "With a friend, eh?"

She looked down at Polpetto, who was now sniffing the garbage bags. "Yes. Just taking this one for a walk."

"He's an energetic beast, *si*?" G said, dropping the bag to pet the dog. "Ah, and he's hungry. I have just the—"

"Don't, please. He just ate. Anything you give him wouldn't be a good idea," she said, when something suddenly occurred to her. G knew just about everyone in town. "G, this is the dog I found at the murder scene yesterday. He might belong to someone who knows what happened to Mimi Catalano. Have you seen him before?"

G stooped closer to get a better look at the dog. He shook his head. "No. Does not look familiar."

She let out a long sigh. "Really? Oh. That's too bad. I thought if anyone knew him, you would."

He took the two bags and one by one tossed them into a dumpster. He said, "You know, you left too soon for me to talk to you. But I heard what Blondie said. You don't have to worry about her."

"Actually, I do. Everyone seems to believe whatever lies she's shilling."

"Nah." He waved a hand dismissively. "I don't. I know Mimi. For years and years, I know her. She was no good."

"You did? So she gave you a hard time, too?"

"No. Not me. She was very friendly to us locals. It's the people from away she has most trouble with. You know, she's the one who came up with the one-euro house deal, years ago."

Audrey squinted at him. "She did? Then why does she have a problem with expats? She must've known that—"

"She was hoping that it would lure back Sicilians who'd moved away. But it backfired on her. And suddenly all these foreigners kept coming in. She didn't like it, so she did everything in her power to give them trouble."

"So you're saying that the person who killed her was probably an expat, and that's why they're focusing on me?"

He shrugged. "I'm saying she wanted to divide people. And maybe she succeeded. There are locals on her side who agree with her, but many locals who don't. Like me. But she has her group of followers who do not like people from outside."

"So you think one of them might be trying to frame me, regardless of who killed her? I heard the beach she was found on is only a ten-minute walk from the city, so really, anyone could have."

"Anything is possible. That beach, I go fishing there, now and then. It is popular with joggers and walkers, but not in the middle of the day. Too hot, even in September. It's very secluded in places, so there is a good chance the police will find no witnesses. It's really a wonder you found the body right away."

"I only did that because of the phone call. Otherwise... who knows?"

"You were with that American, right? That Mason?"

She blinked. Had she said anything to that effect in front of him? Yes, she had, at La Mela Verde the previous night, while talking to Nessa. But G had been so busy serving customers, she hadn't realized he was listening.

What, was *he* jealous? "Yes. He's a friend. And he had a car."

"I'd be careful with him if I were you. I've seen him walking around at night. He looks... very suspicious."

She laughed. "Mason's not suspicious. He's a ladykiller, but not in the way you're thinking."

"I saw him that morning. The morning of the murder. He looked guilty, like he was up to no good."

"What? No, you've got to be mistaken. He was sleeping in that morning."

"No. I am sure I saw him that day." He said it with such zeal that it sent a shiver down Audrey's spine.

"Oh," was all she could say, completely flabbergasted. Was that possible? Why would he have lied to her?

He patted the dog's side. "You two look tired and hungry. Come on in. I make you some of my night's special. *Gambero rosso*."

Audrey was still reeling over the news about Mason. Had he lied to her? And why? G was staring at her, expecting an answer, so she said, "I—I don't know what that is."

"Red prawns. Delicious! I make them with a little lemon juice and olive oil, my specialty. Come …" He motioned them to the back door.

Polpetto started to pull eagerly on his leash, all in, but Audrey stood firm.

"I don't think so. I'm exhausted and not really hungry. It's been a busy day. Plus, I've got to get back to the clinic to drop this guy off and finish up some paperwork. Work has been crazy."

"Hmm. I am sorry about Marco," he said after a few moments. "He did not show up this morning?"

She shook her head.

"Ah. His parents supported Signora Catalano. He told me today he overslept, but …"

"I get it," she said, forcing a smile which turned into a yawn. "It's not his fault. I'll see you later."

Nudging Polpetto so he'd finally take his nose out of a nearby garbage can, she finally got him to continue on his way, back to the clinic.

"I know, boy," she said to him as he led her down the deserted street, his shoulders slumped slightly in defeat. "And I know you probably miss your owner. But we will find him. And we'll get to the bottom of everything else, too."

At least, she hoped. But with all the enemies that this woman had, the only thing Audrey was completely sure about was that *she* hadn't murdered Mimi Catalano. Beyond that, who did was really anyone's guess.

Her first order of business, though, would be finding out exactly why Mason was lying to her.

CHAPTER SIXTEEN

The following morning, Audrey got to the clinic at eight. Her favorite part of her job was the excited chorus of barks and yips and meows all the animals had for her when she went into the kennel. It was music to her ears. She greeted all of them with the annoying, coddling baby-talk Mason hated and got them prepared for the day, letting them out for their daily exercise, cleaning up potty accidents, and replenishing the water bowls.

That took the better part of the hour, but she didn't mind it. This was her paradise. In her element like that, she nearly lost track of time, so when someone knocked on the front door, she expected it to be Mason, reporting for his second day as volunteer.

Instead, it was her first appointment, a woman with a parakeet. It was already nine o'clock. As she flipped the APERTO sign in the front window, let the old lady inside, and told her to make herself comfortable, she peered up and down the street, looking for Mason in all his gorgeousness. But the street was empty.

Odd, she thought, wondering if yesterday's beat-down at the hands of Polpetto had knocked the will out of him.

She also wondered, not for the first time, if there was any truth to what G had said. When he'd answered his door, it looked as though he'd been asleep for hours. Was it really possible that he'd been out that morning? And prowling around at night... well, sure, he was suffering from an abundance of free time, but it wasn't exactly like Mussomeli had a swinging night life. There was no reason for anyone to be combing the streets at night, unless they were up to no good. But ...

No. Not Mason. He was a little bit of a player, but that was about it. Sure, he hated Mimi Catalano, but he wasn't a murderer.

Or was she only thinking that because that was the running assumption? That a beautiful man with such innocent dimples could do no wrong?

She pushed away those thoughts and brought the little parakeet in for his check-up. All good. A perfectly healthy bird, being well cared for by its doting owner, which was what she loved to see.

When she walked the lady to the reception desk, she found Mason sitting behind it, head back against the chair, mouth slightly open. Snoring loudly.

The old lady gasped as he went to scratch his privates. Blushing, Audrey jiggled the chair.

He sprang to his feet. "What? Where am I?" he asked, looking around, alarmed.

"At the vet," she said, trying to play off her annoyance, since customers were there. "Remember?"

"Oh, yeah." He wiped some sleep from his eyes.

"You're late."

He smirked at her. "So, fire me."

Ignoring that, she pointed to her client. "Could you please check Signora Calluci out?" she asked him sternly.

He rubbed more sleep from his eyes as the woman stared at him in disdain. "Yeah. Sure. Got it."

She smiled at the woman. "*Grazie.* Thank you for coming in. All good." She gave a thumbs-up. "Please don't hesitate to call if you need anything."

She put her hand with thumb and forefinger out to her cheek, the international symbol for *Call me,* deciding that rather than doing sign language, she *really* needed to double down on learning Italian. Meanwhile, Mason slumped against the desk like he was about to fall asleep again.

Audrey stomped back to the exam room to clean up, hoping that by making a lot of noise, he wouldn't fall asleep again.

As she scrubbed down the room for the next patient, she kept thinking about what G had said about Mason. She realized she didn't know him, not at all. Other than being from Charleston, he'd been very mum on his life. He'd said he was rich, hadn't he? Maybe he was part of a crime family. What if he'd moved out here to escape some kind of criminal past? He seemed pretty level, but she didn't know. Maybe he had a history of violence. What if he hadn't fully moved beyond his criminal ways, and Mimi Catalano had pushed him too far?

When she finished, she washed her hands and went outside to look for her next patient. But the waiting room was empty. Mason, thankfully, wasn't asleep, but he had an industrial-size thermos of coffee and was chugging it like no tomorrow. "Who is my next appointment?"

He checked the book. "Ricci. A cat."

She looked at the clock on the wall, over the reception desk. "Five minutes late. I wonder if it's another no-show."

"Nah. People around here are always late," he said, yawning again. "Sorry I was late. I had something come up."

His eyes were bleary, like he hadn't gotten any sleep last night. She had to wonder if that was the result of a weight that had been recently thrust upon his shoulders. "It's okay. I'm not paying you. I'm happy you showed up at all," she said lightly, before starting in on the real question: "Is everything okay?"

He nodded. "Yeah. Why wouldn't it be?"

"You just seem really tired, suddenly. Ever since, you know. The thing with Mimi."

He chuckled. "It ain't a guilty conscience, if that's what you're insinuating. Besides, from what I remember, you were the one who woke me up?"

"About that." She leaned her backside against the desk and crossed her arms, trying to choose her words carefully. "Someone said they saw you that morning. And you weren't in bed."

His smile fell. "Who?"

Unable to take the weight of his stare, she looked away. "Well, is it—"

"That boyfriend of yours, huh? What's his name? G?" He shook his head, like, *Figures.* "Of course he'd tell you that. Anything to get me dangling from the hook."

"So it's not true?"

He laughed bitterly and stood up. "I didn't say that. Fine. It's true. I was out that morning. I was out all night, if you need to know. But just because I wasn't in my bed that morning doesn't prove anything." He came up close to her, so close that his warm breath fanned her face. "And I didn't kill the witch, if that's what you're thinking, Boston."

Trapped between him and the desk, she drew back. "I didn't... I mean, I didn't say that—"

"But that's what you thought. Admit it."

She stood there, trembling, unable to say a word. No, she didn't know much about Mason at all. She didn't know he could be this intense. The fire in his eyes was enough to incinerate her. Had he snapped and gone all intense on Mimi, too? Looking at him now, it didn't seem like that much of a stretch.

But almost the second that fire ignited, it started to burn out. His eyes softened, and he raked his hands through his hair as he let out a tired sigh. "Fine. Don't. But then you don't want possible suspects working for you either. It could cramp your style."

He grabbed his mug of coffee and stalked for the door.

"Wait. You're not leaving, are you?"

He turned around. "But that's all this town is. Possible suspects. So good luck finding more help."

She shook her head. "Wait! That's not what I said. I don't want you to—"

But before she could finish her sentence, he'd already stormed out the door.

Before she could run after him, she got a phone call. Still rattled, she forgot her normal business greeting: "Yes?"

"Is this Dottore Smart?"

She cleared her throat. "Oh. Um, yes. Is this Mr. Falco?"

"That's right. I wanted to stop by the clinic today and see how it has been going, but it doesn't look like I'll be able to make it. So how are things?"

She shrugged. "It's good. Busy, like I mentioned. I'm getting strays in, handling appointments. There is definitely mange going around, but we'll get it under control, little by little. Have you heard anything about that tax?"

"Nothing official. Several people on the board have indicated it might be dead, without Mimi to back it up. So… fingers crossed."

"That would be amazing. I'll keep thinking good thoughts. I know you said that the budget's tight, but is there any possibility of hiring extra help, now that …" She didn't want to say, *Now that Mimi Catalano is gone,* but she'd been wondering constantly if it would improve her situation at all.

"Yes. There is a possibility. I will definitely bring it up. And I do think I may be able to squeeze more money out of the board."

Audrey smiled. "Really? That's good."

"Yes. Mimi Catalano's death was a terrible thing, but I can't pretend that it didn't feel like a weight has been lifted off of me. Much of the council says the same. But she did have her backers, and I'm not sure their numbers. I will keep you posted."

Her smile faded when she realized that as much as he'd been worried about her, he, too, had a motive. "Have the police questioned you?"

"Oh, yes. Extensively," he said, sounding exhausted. "But it is good. They need to. I, luckily, have an alibi. I was in a meeting downtown so I have several witnesses to corroborate that."

"That's good. I'm jealous. I wish I had the same." She wished Mason had the same, too. At first she'd been sure G had to have been mistaken. Mason had been sleeping that morning. He wasn't a murderer. But with the way he'd just acted… she had to admit, it was definitely suspicious.

"Don't worry. I was speaking to Detective DiNardo, and he's making strides in the case. There are quite a few leads he's pursuing."

"That's the problem. There are too many leads. I have to imagine that it must be mind-boggling, sifting through all the information. Half the town probably had a beef with her."

"Yes. Well. Get some sleep. I'm sure you'll be busy tomorrow."

She wished him good night and hung up the phone. As she did, she thought of Polpetto. The police were so busy pursuing their many leads, they really hadn't been very interested in him at all. Which was crazy, when she stopped to think of it. Polpetto had been there, on the beach. He was, quite possibly, the most important witness of all.

A thought occurred to her, one she knew Mason would disapprove of, knowing how silly he'd thought she was for wanting to go to the beach alone. But what was he, her warden? Besides, she'd tried to tell the police. They hadn't listened. By the time she'd snuggled into bed, it was more like a demand.

If they aren't going to try to use Polpetto for what he knows, maybe I can.

CHAPTER SEVENTEEN

After her last appointment left at four, Audrey set to giving the strays their afternoon care. When she finished, she looked at Polpetto.

"If only you could talk," she said to him, stroking behind his ears. "Then you could tell me what you know, and I wouldn't be going around accusing my friends of murder."

But now that she had the time, maybe there was a way to get Polpetto to finally reveal what he knew.

By finding his owner, whoever *that* was.

Polpetto was big, a good-looking dog. Memorable. He was a pet that any owner would've proudly shown off. She understood if Mason hadn't had any luck tracking down the owner. He was new to Mussomeli. But it was strange that someone like G, who knew just about everyone in town, had never seen the dog. To her, that meant it was likely the dog wasn't even from the city.

But she was out of ideas. And whoever owned him had taken very good care of him, which meant that he'd taken him to another vet, showed him off. Other people had to know him.

Poor Polpetto. She sensed a sadness behind his eyes, like he missed the twenty-four-seven attention his owner had given him. Even if the owner didn't know anything about the murder, the least she could do was try to reunite them.

"Okay, baby," she said to him as she brought him to her office and sat down behind her computer. "I know what we need to do."

While Polpetto curled up in the corner of the room, Audrey set about creating FOUND DOG posters. She used Google translate, hoping she had the Italian wording right, and placed a photograph of Polpetto in the very center. On the bottom, she wrote: *Inquire at Dott. Smart Veterinary Clinic, Via Barcellona, Mussomeli.* Then she printed out one hundred copies of the flyer and grabbed her stapler.

"You ready, Polpetto, my boy?" she asked him, clipping his leash on his collar and stuffing the flyers under her arm. "Let's go find your human!"

He excitedly sprang into action, dragging her out the door and down the street, much like before. She could barely get him to stop long enough to affix a poster to the sides of buildings and lampposts.

He seemed to want to take her in an entirely different path than she'd been before, which didn't help her determine the owner's neighborhood at all.

A couple posters later, she was completely out of breath and exhausted. At that point, she thought she'd go back to the clinic, but Polpetto had other ideas. He started dragging her down a secluded, wooded path, away from the city. It contained a number of long switchbacks, heading down, down, down… to the bottom of the hillside. Though she could only see portions of the path from where she stood, it seemed like it went on forever.

"Whoa," she said breathlessly to him, not that it helped. "What goes down has to go back up again, and I think you're going to give me a heart attack if I have to climb up here again."

Ignoring her, he barreled along, down numerous stone steps, making Audrey slip on the loose gravel of the path, until she nearly slid onto her backside. At that point, she grabbed the leash hard. Finally, Polpetto slowed.

"I know you're excited, boy," she said to him, trying to get him to heel. "But this path is literally my worst nightmare. You sure do love your walk, don't you?"

He licked her hand and nodded down the path. She took that as a yes.

But she had to admit, the view from here was pretty breathtaking. Mussomeli was atop a hill, with precarious drops in all directions. From here, she could see miles and miles of green hillsides and small villages, stretching all the way out, almost to the Mediterranean. The sun was bright. The air was cool and yet not cold, and in it, she could almost smell the sea.

"All right, I forgive you for taking me on this Death March. This is some pretty scenery," she said.

When she stepped a bit off the path, onto a rock, she looked down and saw a thin swath of dark blue water, sparkling in the setting sun. It looked familiar.

She peered closer. Was this… yes. This had to be the path that led to the lake that Detective DiNardo had told her about. Clearly, Polpetto had taken it many a time.

Squinting in the dying light, she noticed a few people walking on the beach below. Was that the beach where she'd found Mimi? Police officers, dressed all in blue. They appeared to be moving slowly, combing the area for clues. As she looked closer, she realized that one of the men, in a dark blazer, was Detective DiNardo.

The wind on this outcropping was especially fierce, almost pushing her in the direction of the beach, so even without Polpetto, she felt compelled to finish the walk. She sucked in a breath and slipped her way down the rest of the way, to level ground. Walking along the narrow path, between scrubby bushes and olive trees, she arrived on the sandy beach. Polpetto barked at the officers and dragged her along.

DiNardo looked up just as the monstrous dog was about to pounce on him. He quickly backed up as Audrey tugged on the leash, finally succeeding in getting Polpetto under control.

"Crime scene!" he shouted at her, annoyed. "Didn't you see the tape?"

"There wasn't any tape!" she said, scanning the area. Yes, there was bright yellow tape around the perimeter, but it disappeared before it got to the opening she'd come out of. Someone must've ripped it down.

Audrey winced. The light was dying, so she hadn't seen, but it was a good chance the culprit was Polpetto, who'd been rushing so far ahead of her, willing to flatten any obstacle in his way.

The detective whistled to one of his officers and yelled something in Italian to him, motioning to the opening. The officer ran ahead and began to take care of it.

"Back up," he said to her.

She did, though it wasn't easy. Polpetto didn't understand yellow crime scene tape. All he wanted was his walk. She finally got him to obey and come behind the tape. "Sorry."

"What brings you down here?" he asked, his tone more relaxed. "Sorry if I snapped. We've been discouraging nosy observers all day long."

"So you've had a lot of people around here?"

He nodded and reached down to pet Polpetto. Polpetto kept pulling on the leash, growling a bit. He had his sights set on his path, apparently, and would not go down without a fight. "It's normal. People are very macabre. But it interferes with the investigation."

"I'm sure," she said, rolling her shoulder. Her arm ached from trying to hold the mastiff back.

He pointed to the remaining flyers under her arm. "Lost dog?"

"Polpetto was the dog I found on this beach," she said. "Remember? I was wondering if his owner might have anything to do with the murder."

DiNardo shook his head. "No. There are dozens of strays prowling this beach. Likely, that dog has no owner."

"He did once," Audrey said. "He's very well trained and well cared for."

"Perhaps. But as you know, the town is overrun by strays. This beach is a popular spot for them. If this dog had an owner, they likely left him here when they moved out of town. Many of these poor strays, unfortunately, once belonged to families."

Oh. She hadn't thought of that. That dashed her hopes of Polpetto leading her to the killer. "But he seemed to know right where Mimi's body was. He led us there, like Lassie."

He stared at her, eyebrows raised. Apparently, that wasn't enough to convince him that Polpetto was in any way a key witness to the events that had transpired on this beach. Meanwhile, next to her, Polpetto continued to growl, a low, aching rumble.

"Shush, Polpetto," she whispered, trying to calm him as she wrapped the leash around her wrist one more time. "Well, do you have any other leads?"

"We have quite a few of them. It's not being made any easier by the fact that everyone knows someone who had a motive."

"But very few people actually have the nerve to attack a person like that in broad daylight. Knock her over the head with a rock while she was out walking? That's kind of gutsy, don't you think?"

"The coroner isn't convinced that is indeed what happened," he said with a shrug. "She might have gotten into an altercation with someone. Maybe she was shoved, stumbled backward, and hit her head on a rock. There really is no evidence right now to say which."

So that means, forget about being "the murdering type." It could be anyone, Audrey thought. *No wonder they think it might be me. It could be a woman.*

And it could be Mason, too.

Before she could reply, Polpetto somehow shook loose of the collar she'd put on him. She reached for him, but only managed to touch his furry backside as he tore off in the direction of the lake.

"Polpetto! Wait!" she cried as he bounded off, kicking up sand in his exuberant run.

DiNardo groaned.

"Sorry." She held up the leash. "I don't know how he got out. I can go ..."

Before she could finish, he lifted the tape for her to pass underneath.

"Thanks. Sorry again," she said, rushing down the beach toward the dog. Thankfully, he'd gotten only halfway toward the water when he stopped. Now, he was digging with all his might, sending sand flying into the air in a white cloud.

"Hey. Cut it out!" she said to him as sand blasted against her cheeks. "Chill!"

The dog listened to her, miraculously. The second she arrived at the massive hole he'd dug, he dipped his muzzle in and pulled something out. He laid it down on Audrey's feet; something red and leather, covered in drool and sand.

Audrey crouched to pick it up. A dog collar.

"Is this yours, boy?" she asked him, wiping the sand from the item. It was well-constructed, heavy, and real leather, and likely had cost quite a bit of money. There was a tag hanging from it. All it said on it was *Tito*. "Tito?"

The dog barked.

"Is that your name? Tito?"

DiNardo approached just as the dog was barking again. "Tito. It means giant."

Giant? She wrinkled her nose. *How unoriginal.* Over the past few days, she'd come to think of him as nothing but *Polpetto*. Polpetto, her little meatball of joy. "So I guess he's not a stray."

He rubbed his jaw and nodded. "I'd say not."

She held the collar out to him. "Do you want this? As evidence?"

DiNardo shook his head. "No, the dog's not important. There really is nothing tying that collar, or the dog, to the crime. You might as well take it. And you'd better get back up to town with this rascal. It's starting to get dark."

Audrey nodded and said goodbye, then dragged the dog up to the pathway up to town, out of breath and panting. Her mind spun with potential scenarios. Maybe Polpetto had fought with the assailant and lost his collar in the scuffle? Maybe the killer had torn the collar from Polpetto so that no one would know who his owner was? Maybe …

She threw herself down on a rock at the side of the path, lungs burning. Polpetto laid his head in her lap as if to say, *How can I help?*

"You can learn to speak English," she whispered to him. "Because I have a feeling you know more than anyone."

Audrey had nearly made it to the top of the pathway leading up to the city when the sun slipped down behind the buildings of Mussomeli, towering in the distance. She fanned herself, wishing she'd brought a bottle of water. Her throat was bone dry and her lungs were still screaming for mercy.

She took a few more steps, wavering in her exhaustion, when she heard footsteps approaching rapidly behind her.

CHAPTER EIGHTEEN

A shiver went down Audrey's back as the presence behind her bore down on her.

She jumped, getting into defensive posture—arms raised, legs ready to run— as a dark blur swept by her on the path.

A voice called out to her with an American accent, "Better get moving. This path gets dark when the sun goes down, and even that horse isn't going to save you from the wild boars. They feast on human blood."

Wild boars? She looked around, alarmed, then realized the voice sounded familiar.

"Nessa?"

Thank god. It was probably the first time Audrey'd been *glad* to see the woman. Of course, Nessa was always out running, morning, noon, and night. And she usually headed off this way. So it made total sense that this was the path she took during her jaunts. It was a popular route for runners.

She slowed to a stop and turned around, still jogging in place. She was wearing a barely there bra top and shorts that accentuated her tanned, fit body and rippling abs. She didn't seem winded at all, which Audrey guessed made sense, since the girl *lived* to run. "Oh, and I saw a rattlesnake on that rock the other day."

Audrey jumped to her feet as if a rocket had been launched under her butt. "I was just on my way up."

Nessa rolled her eyes. "Sure you were. You look like you're dying."

And I'm sure you'd be happy about that, Audrey thought, following her. She expected that Nessa would turn around and continue her run, but instead, Nessa pulled out her earbuds and started to stretch. "So what were you trying to do? Return to the scene of the crime?"

"Ha, ha. You're very funny. You know I had nothing to do with that murder. First of all, I just proved to you I can't get down there without giving myself a few near coronaries."

"I don't know anything of the sort. This can all be an act," she said, hitching one shoulder as she pulled her foot behind her, to her backside.

Next to her, Polpetto growled suspiciously. Good dog. Audrey had always been one to believe that dogs had a sixth sense when it came to people's character. In mere minutes, he'd somehow caught on that Nessa wasn't a nice person, something that would probably take most humans a lifetime to realize.

She stared at the collar in her hands, trying to think. *Anyone could have killed Mimi Catalano and ripped this leash from Polpetto,* she thought.

Tito. Whatever.

Suddenly, something occurred to her. *Right. The murderer could be absolutely anyone.*

"I was actually down there because I was thinking of taking up running," she said. Nessa had begun walking toward her house, and even though the road was now more level, Audrey had to rush to keep up. "You think you can give me any tips?"

Nessa gave her a sideways look. "No. Well, one. Don't go running that path. It's much too advanced for beginners."

"Oh. So you run down there every day?"

"*Twice* a day," she said proudly. "Morning and night. I run down to the lake and do the loop. It's about seven miles. Like I said, not for beginners."

"Wow," Audrey said, thinking to herself, *Morning. If she'd run there in the morning, then she very well could've been there and seen Polpetto. Not only that, she could've also seen the murderer.* "That's impressive. You're obviously very fit."

She smiled. "Well, the camera adds ten pounds. And I need to look good for the filming," she said, fluffing her ponytail. "It starts in two weeks. And like I said, you're welcome to be part of episode seven. We need filler. Don't worry about being frumpy, though …most of the time, the camera will be on me. So it doesn't matter too much what you look like."

Audrey stared at her, a fake smile plastered on her face. Truthfully, she'd sooner get dental work. "Um. Yeah. Maybe?"

"Come on, Audrey. Don't be all wishy washy. I mean, it's the opportunity of a lifetime. Most people would kill to be on national television, even if it will make them look fat," she said. "I mean, that hot boy Mason jumped at the chance. As most people would. Not that that boy has any fat at all on him at all. Yum."

She asked Mason? Audrey didn't know why her stomach swam at the thought of the two of them talking. They were on the edge of town now, not far from their street, surrounded by scrubby bushes and the low stone wall that surrounded most of the city proper. Audrey's legs ached to take her there, because they wanted a seat. "I'll think about it. So... were you running on Tuesday, this week?"

"Of course. I ran every day this week."

"In the morning?"

"Yes."

"On the path by the lakeside?"

"Yes." She stopped walking. "What's this all about? I told you, that's not a good path for a beginner... Wait."

Audrey looked up just in time to see Nessa's eyes widen. She'd made the connection.

"What are you thinking? That I had anything to do with that woman's death?" She snorted.

"Well, maybe you didn't. But maybe you saw someone there who looked suspicious?"

Nessa crossed her arms. "No, I didn't. If you really want to know what happened to that woman, you should ask your big dog there. He probably saw more than I did."

Suddenly, something clicked in Audrey's brain. Something was off. "Wait. How did you know that this was the dog I found on the beach?" The pieces of the puzzle started to fall into place. "I don't think I said anything about that. In fact, I know I didn't."

Nessa's face, which was simply glistening with a post-run glow, began to turn bright red. Without another word, she turned toward her house and dashed away.

"Nessa!" Audrey called, rushing after her. This time, it must've been adrenaline, because somehow, Audrey was able to match her pace.

Nessa tried to slam the door in Audrey's face, but Polpetto was too quick, and far too strong. He pushed open the door and pinned the waifish woman against the wall of her front hallway, drooling heavily on her abs.

"Ugh!" she cried, heaving great big breaths as she tried to flatten herself and hold up her hands to protect herself. "Down, boy! Ew, drool! Audrey! Call off your freakishly mammoth-sized mutant hellhound!"

"One second," Audrey gasped, doubling over, trying to catch her breath.

It kind of sucked that Nessa, after seven miles, wasn't even winded, and Audrey felt like she was about to die.

Finally, she managed to gasp out, "Not until you let me know what you're hiding."

Wincing, Nessa began to sob. "Okay! Okay, fine! Just stop it from slobbering all over me!"

Audrey didn't get what the big deal was. Nessa had been running, so she was covered in sweat as it was. Wasn't her first order of business a shower anyway? She tugged on Polpetto's leash. "Okay, that's enough, boy," she said to him, and obediently, he followed her commands, retreating behind her legs.

Nessa scowled at her. "You're lucky I don't call the police on you. That's harassment. Or... something. You could go to jail for that."

"If you have anything to do with Mimi Catalano's death, you'd be pretty silly to want to involve the police," Audrey warned.

"I *don't*," she snapped, grabbing a towel off a hook in the entryway. She carefully swabbed up the drool, still grimacing. "But your horse and I have been acquainted."

"Really? How?"

Nessa peered outside. An old lady was pushing a squeaky-wheeled cart down the street, but Nessa eyed her as if she was a government spy. "Oh. Stop hovering in the doorway like some dowdy vampire and just come in," she muttered.

Audrey stepped farther into the house. She'd never been invited into Nessa's place, but knowing all the work she'd had done, and the fact that Nessa was an interior designer "of great renown," Audrey expected the place to be a showroom. And she was right. The walls were painted a pale terra-cotta color, and the furnishings looked like a cover of *Better Homes and Gardens*. It had that distinctly unlived-in feeling, of a piece of real estate that was set up to be attractive to a buyer. Nevertheless, Audrey sighed a little, wistfully. Her house was a complete shambles compared to this.

Nessa might have had the perfect house for hostessing, but she was not in any way, shape, or form a hostess. When Audrey and Polpetto were finally inside, she slammed the door and said, "Yes, I saw that animal—" She looked down at it and clenched her teeth. "God! Is that normal for that thing to drool that much?"

She threw her towel on the travertine tile floor and moved it under the flow of Polpetto's drool with one sneakered foot.

Satisfied, she said, "Yes, I saw that animal. He was on the beach, and he was making such a racket, howling like crazy, I thought he might be injured. So I called you."

It took a moment for the words to sink in, for Audrey to understand what she was saying. That phone call… *Nessa* had made it? Nessa, who loved nothing more than herself, was concerned about an animal? Audrey didn't buy it.

"*You* called me?" Audrey said, mouth hanging slightly open. "You were the one who disguised your voice? Why?"

She shrugged. "I didn't want you to know it was me. Duh."

"Why?"

"Because then you would've asked me to stay on the premises and wait for you to arrive and I have better things to do."

That was true. She would have. "But …did you see Mimi?"

"Actually, I did. I passed her on my way down to the lake loop. She was going really slow because she was wearing heels. That's why I remember her. I thought that was a dumb choice for that hill." She went to a floating shelf and arranged a little potted plant there. "Then I ran the loop, and I didn't see anyone else. When I was about to come back up, that's when I saw the dog. Stupid thing attacked me."

"And?"

"And then it ran off. I heard it let out a whine, which made me think it'd gotten hurt. That's when I called you."

"So you didn't see anyone else down there? Are you sure?"

"Yes, I'm sure," she snapped, giving Audrey a hard stare. "Well, I saw one guy, but I only got a glimpse of him. He was tall. But not Mason-tall. This guy was big and bulky. He was wearing like a hat, I think. He was down by the water, so I thought he was fishing, but probably not, because I didn't see a pole."

Audrey gnawed on her lip. That description would fit half the men in Mussomeli. "Is that all you remember? Think, Nessa."

"Yeah. Sorry. That's it. Like I said, I only got a glimpse of him. What are you, Nancy Drew? Why are you asking all these questions?"

"I don't know. Maybe because… for some reason I can't quite put my finger on… the police somehow think I did it? It may have something to do with you shouting it from the highest peak in Mussomeli?"

She laughed bitterly. "Hmm. Did you?"

Audrey sighed and turned to leave. "You know, you're the only witness. If your story is true, you should go to the police."

"What do you mean, *if*? Of course it's true. And I was going to. When I had time."

"Right. I know, you have such a busy schedule, getting all those runs in," Audrey muttered as she reached for the doorknob.

"Like I said, got to look good for my public. We're talking national television, Audrey. It's *that* important." She drew her bottom lip under her teeth and gave Audrey a guilty look. "And... if I'm the only one who witnessed it, that puts me pretty close to the murder. I don't want them to god forbid, suspect me, or anything."

"Yeah. The horror," Audrey said, nudging Polpetto's leash. She stepped outside and closed the door, thinking.

Now we just need to look for a tall, bulky man in a hat. Sure. That'll be easy-peasy.

But if that's what it took to find the killer, she was game. She was ready to scour the entire town if she had to.

CHAPTER NINETEEN

It was well after dark when Audrey finally returned to the clinic to drop off Polpetto. As he neared the doorway, he whined a little, tugging at her heartstrings.

She crouched down in front of him. "Look, boy. I know you want your owner. I know you miss him. You want to belong with someone. But the signs are up. Hopefully, you won't have to wait too long."

As she brought him inside, she entertained the idea of bringing him into her own home, in the event his owner was never found. That was the danger in being a vet. Back at her Boston apartment, there had been a strict no-pets rule, which she abided by, as much as it killed her, because her finances wouldn't permit otherwise. But here, with the opportunity to take in any stray that caught her fancy, there was a definite chance of having her place overrun by animals... and quickly. Her bleeding heart was just too soft, and she had a hard time looking into the eyes of those needy animals and saying no.

But Nick hadn't exactly gotten along with Polpetto when they were introduced. That was a problem.

Besides, she'd been making a little money, now, to pay back some of her debts, but she really couldn't afford another mouth to feed just yet. Especially one that ate as much as Polpetto did.

"Don't worry, you'll be fine," she said, as much to herself as to the dog as she brought Polpetto in and let him off the leash. She looked at the collar in her hands. It was heavy. Expensive. Definitely the mark of someone who cared for their pets. "I bet someone is missing you, too."

The clinic had only been open a few days, and she already had twelve strays. She hadn't even looked that much, really. She'd been planning to organize a community-wide pet adoption day, especially for when space was at a premium, and now that was looking like it would have to happen sooner rather than later.

As she finished taking care of the rest of the animals, she tried to focus on the pet adoption day. On a weekend, probably. She'd waive the application fee for applicants with good homes. All the standard things. That was about as far as she got before someone started rapping on her door. Even though the sign on the door said the clinic was closed, someone had likely seen her moving through the big storefront window.

Hands buried to the elbow in rubber gloves for cleaning the kennels, she went to the window and found Orlando Falco. She held up a finger and peeled them off, then twisted the lock and opened it for him.

"I'm sorry to bother you again after hours, but after hours is all I seem to get. You are a very busy person, too, I see," he remarked, holding out a bottle of red wine. "A gift for you."

"Oh, thank you! There's always something to do here at Hotel Smart," she said with a smile, studying the label, which was in Italian, circa 2017. "How are you?"

"I'm well, thank you," he said, but she could tell from the three very pronounced wrinkles on his forehead that something was wrong. "May I come in and speak with you a moment?"

"Sure." She pushed aside the door to allow him to pass through. The reception area was a little messy, with magazines and adoption brochures scattered about, so she started to gather them together while he looked around the place. "What can I help you with?"

"It looks good in here. You have been doing a wonderful job."

She stopped and looked at him. Why did she get the feeling he was stalling to avoid telling her some bad news? "Thanks …" She sensed a *but*, even though she didn't say it.

"Anyway." He clutched his briefcase in front of him with both hands. "I've just gotten done speaking to a few of the other councilmen about our meeting tomorrow. First on the docket is the tax on strays that Mimi Catalano was pushing."

"Right, but you said that you thought it might be dead?"

"Well, it appears I could be wrong." He pressed his lips together hard, as if trying to think of the best way to phrase his next words. "Several of the other council people think it's a good idea that has merit."

"What? Are you kidding me?" She tossed the magazines down on the coffee table and dragged both hands down her face. "I thought we had a good chance."

"I thought so, too. Of course, I'm going to argue on your behalf. But the best I can do is state our case, and hope that they see our side." He shrugged. "I wish I could do more. I'm sure the news won't help you rest easy, but I thought you should know."

"No, I'm glad you did. And I don't think there's anything more you could do," Audrey said, slinking down into one of the chairs in the waiting room. "I'll just have to get more paying clients in. The kennels are already filling up. I was planning a pet adoption day for one of the weekends coming up, but is it even worthwhile? I'm assuming the tax is going to be passed on to anyone who adopts one of these strays. It's going to make adoption out of reach for people, I'm afraid."

He shook his head. "We might be surprised. I think you should go along with the plans. And I'll see what I can do to drum up support among the local businesses and homes, even if it isn't monetary in nature. What else do you need?"

"Old blankets and towels would be very helpful. If anyone has any pet food or supplies left over, I'll take it. Newspapers. Whatever." She was babbling now, so tired she could barely think. But she got the feeling she wouldn't be able to sleep at all tonight. Not with the threat of that tax coming. "I'll just try to make do as best as I can. I appreciate all your help."

"You're welcome," he said, moving for the door. He opened it and nodded at her. *"Buona notte."*

"Good night," she called after him, but it felt like anything but. She placed a hand over her chest. It felt like her heart was on the verge of breaking. It was one thing to fail on her own. But all those poor rescues would be out on the street again, fending for their lives, if she didn't find some way to make this work.

The only problem was, she couldn't think of anything more she could do to scrimp and save. If that tax went through, she couldn't see any way that the clinic would succeed.

CHAPTER TWENTY

When Audrey got home, she expected to find Nick waiting for her, as he usually was. The fox followed her around everywhere, but he always knew that at a certain point in the night, Audrey would return home and give him his dinner, and a few apples as a treat.

But she found a very different sort of creature outside her door.

It was Mason, standing at the front stoop with what looked like a red Tupperware container.

Before she could get all excited that he was waiting for her, with something that looked very much like a peace offering, a high-pitched laugh erupted from across the narrow street.

As she came closer, Mason said something, but it wasn't directed at her. More giggles.

Nessa. He was talking to… no, *flirting with* Nessa.

Drawing closer, she heard Nessa say, in a high airy voice the woman never used when speaking to Audrey, "So it's a plan? You'll really *spice* up my episode two!"

"Sure, I'm there," Mason replied coolly, as his eyes wandered to and landed on Audrey. He cleared his throat. "Hey."

"Hey," she replied tersely, moving past him toward the door. She opened it quickly, scanning around the doorstep, and sighed, annoyed.

She slipped inside and went to close the door on him, but he put a hand out before she could. The heavy door bounced off his forearm. "Ow. Frick! You trying to kill me? I brought you a hot brown."

Audrey winced. She hadn't meant to close it that hard. "A what?"

He held it up, still shaking his other arm. "A hot brown. Recipe from back home. I made it for dinner but I wasn't all that hungry."

"That's nice, but …" She went out to the front stoop and looked around. Thankfully, Nessa had gone back inside. But Nick was nowhere to be found. Her shoulders slumped. He'd probably find his way home, but she didn't want him getting into any trouble.

"What's bothering you?"

"Nothing. Just that you probably scared Nick away. He usually meets me at the clinic or is waiting for me when I get home. And with you there, he probably…" She finally looked at him. "How long were you waiting out here?"

"Ah, just about …" He checked his phone. "An hour?"

Her eyes widened. "An hour?"

"Hot brown's cold. Sorry."

Her heart softened to him at once, as if he was one of her pathetic strays. "No, that's okay!" She took it from his hands. "That's so nice. I'm actually starving."

"Yeah. I figured you were gonna put in a long day, especially without help," he said, with a guilty shrug.

As she was about to close the door, Nick squeezed through. She smiled as he jumped into her arms, and nuzzled his soft fur. "Yeah. It was pretty long. I'm exhausted."

Mason watched with a bit of disgust on his face, but offered no comment. He pointed to the door. "Well, I won't keep you. I just came to—"

Why did Mason leaving feel like the end of the world? "No! Stay. I just got this wine as a gift. Want some?" she asked a little desperately.

He shrugged. "Never could turn down good wine. From an admirer?"

She let out one of her nervous giggles, but cut it short. The last thing she needed was to deteriorate into a crushing teenager around him, especially after she'd made such strides away from her old self.

But it *was* nice to know he thought she had admirers. And did she detect a little jealousy? *No need for that, Mason, dear. You don't know who you're talking to.*

"From Orlando Falco," she said, heading into the kitchen, where she brought down two stemless wine glasses and opened drawers, looking for the corkscrew. "He also brought the news that the council's voting on that stray tax, and there's a good chance it's going to go through. I think he was hoping to soften the blow for me."

"You're kidding," he said, sliding down into a chair at her bistro table. "Even with the old bag dead?"

"Yep. Seems like she had a bunch of friends who want to honor her name by carrying out her last wishes or something," Audrey said, handing him his glass of wine. She took a big gulp of hers and sat down in front of the food container. She peeled off the top and sniffed. "Mmmm. This smells good."

"You could heat it up in the—"

He stopped when she took it in her hands, opened her mouth wide, and took a massive bite. Chewing, her eyes widened. "Mmmm. Dish ish goo."

"I know. Old family recipe. Had to make some substitutions but it gave it a Sicilian flavor."

She finished chewing and licked the grease off her fingers. "Amazing. Who knew you could cook?"

"One of my many talents." He sipped the wine. "You look like hell, you know."

Audrey smoothed down her hair. Great. Just the kind of compliment she was looking for.

"Well, I've been a little busy, if my eating dinner at ten o'clock at night hasn't tipped you off," she said, doing her best to disguise her hurt as she took a tomato out of the sandwich and stuffed it into her mouth. Maybe it was that she hadn't had anything since the early morning granola bar, but this was quite possibly the best sandwich she'd ever had, cold or not. She scanned the bleak kitchen. She'd had all these plans to make it nice and homey, and other than the homey gingham curtains, she hadn't done much at all. There was a power sander, sitting in the middle of the floor. "And the house looks like *crap*."

"It'll get there."

"I guess. Eventually."

"Hey. Why not right now?" He pointed to the sander and slipped to his knees. Nick scampered around him, thinking he wanted to play, but Mason politely nudged him off, surveying the floor. "You need to even this out?"

"What are you doing?" she cried in alarm. "I mean, I thought I should even it before I put the tile down. I didn't do it in the bathroom and it's kind of lumpy. But not at ten at night."

"Eh. In Charleston, it's early," he said, grabbing the sander and getting to work.

She set some apples out for Nick and watched him, trying not to feel like a voyeur, but the way his back muscles strained underneath his T-shirt and his biceps bulged, it was hard to tear her eyes away. He did about a quarter of the floor while she polished off her dinner.

He turned off the sander and checked his phone. "I've got to go. But if you want to leave a spare key for me, I can come in and finish later."

She stared at him. He said it almost as if he had somewhere to be, which made her suspicious. Where was he going at night? "Thanks, but—"

"And if you don't think I'm fouling things up too much at the clinic, I'm happy to come in and help there."

"But… I thought you hated those animals."

"They're not that bad. And I'm bored. I was going to keep working on my house but then I got notice that my plans are still under review, even with that Catalano woman gone. So I've got nothing to do. And I'm …" He stopped, as if there was something he wasn't sure he should say. "Truth is, I don't start things I don't mean to finish. And I shouldn't have walked out on you." He looked uncharacteristically sheepish and unsure of himself, darting his eyes away from hers.

She smiled. "It was my fault. I shouldn't have suspected you. I know you're not a murderer. So feel free to stop buttering me up by doing all these nice things for me."

He went to the door. "You find out who that big creature belongs to?"

"Nope. The police don't think he has anything to do with the murder. They say there are strays all over. But I get the feeling the police don't have much else to go on. They were on the beach earlier today, trying to find more clues." She yawned, simply thinking of that long, tiring walk back up to town.

"Well. I'll see you, Boston. Try not to worry too much about everything," he said, waving before slipping out the door.

Try not to worry? With everything I have to worry about, she thought, looking around the ruins of her hardly begun reno, *I'm going to be up all night.*

*

Audrey was wrong.

She fell asleep nearly the second she settled into bed, and though in the back of her mind, she knew she was dreaming, she was too tired to wake herself.

Why else would her father be there, walking through the empty house with her, shaking his head at all the mess? "What have you been up to, Audrey?" he said. "I thought you'd have been much further along than this."

"I'm trying," she said. "I'm busy."

But suddenly, the walls of her Sicilian home fell away, and she was standing in the grand, magnificent two-story foyer of an old, stately mansion overlooking the Back Bay in Boston. Her father's last renovation attempt. She was thirteen, and up to that point, she'd been her father's right hand. All the other girls at school, Brina included, no longer liked hanging out with their parents, but Audrey didn't care. She still followed him around, stopping by whatever house he was renovating on the way home from school, wanting to make herself useful.

Now, she stood in that massive home, surrounded by unpainted drywall and unfinished wainscotting, the distinct scent of sawdust and paint heavy in her nostrils. The house was dark. "Dad?" she asked, looking around for any sign of him. He usually left his favorite toolbox someplace in the homes he renovated. Last she'd seen it, the night before, it'd been on the kitchen island.

But now it was gone.

The night before, he'd seemed strange. Off. He hadn't been angry, just sad, maybe. He'd taken her out for ice cream, just the two of them, even though it was a school night. He hadn't spoken much. The only thing she remembered was him telling her to do well in school, get good grades, and maybe one day, she could be a vet, like she always wanted.

"Dad?" she called again, her voice echoing across the dark expanse of the unfinished house. "Dad?"

She went from room to room, opening and passing through door after door, each one getting smaller and smaller, until she found herself trapped. So trapped, she couldn't even breathe …

Audrey sat bolt upright in bed and looked around, breathing hard. It took her a moment to recognize the walls of her Sicilian home and remember she was no longer in Boston.

That house. It'd been almost twenty years since she'd been in there, and though it was likely a gorgeous showpiece of Boston's Back Bay now, it still made her shudder, as if it was some haunted house. She'd gone through every room in that house, looking for her father, fearing the worst. By the end, sobbing, she'd gone home.

That was when her mother told her that her father had moved out. Gone across country, or something. Left them.

No note. No goodbye. No nothing.

She'd always been Daddy's girl. It wasn't that she didn't believe her mother; she simply thought she knew her father better. At least, she knew that he would never simply abandon her. So seeking confirmation, she'd gone to their bedroom and opened the closet. His side had been cleared out—flannel shirts, jeans, sneakers and work boots, even the suit he'd worn to her middle school graduation. Everything gone.

Except, she'd drawn him a picture, a long time ago. Probably when she was in kindergarten, or maybe slightly afterward. The two of them, just stick figures, really, in front of one of his amazing houses, hammers and screwdrivers in hand. It'd stared back at her from the inside of the closet door. He hadn't taken that.

Settling into bed, she gathered Nick to her chest and stroked his fur, thinking she wouldn't be able to fall asleep again, after that.

Again, thankfully, she was wrong.

But this time, she dreamed of Mimi's body, lying in the sand, and the mysterious tall man in a hat, who was still at large… and quite possibly, a murderer.

CHAPTER TWENTY ONE

Audrey was pretty sure that hot brown would've made a nice home for itself in her stomach, and she wouldn't be hungry the following day. But she wasn't just hungry that morning when she woke up. She was *ravenous*.

Maybe it had been that amazing sandwich, making her stomach go, "More please!" but she thought of Mason the whole way over to La Mela Verde. Of course, he could cook. Was there anything he didn't do well?

And the way he'd gotten down to business, sanding her floor? Not only that, but she kept thinking of what he'd said to her, in her kitchen, with that sheepish look between his dimples. *I don't start anything I don't mean to finish.*

If there was one quality Audrey valued above all others, it was that. Probably because of her dad. After last night, she no longer believed Mason was a killer. In fact… quite the opposite. She had to admit, she was feeling… feelings for him. Ones she didn't really like.

Stop it, Audrey. Like you need to complicate your life any more by adding another unrequited love to the mix?

She went inside the café and slipped onto her favorite stool. Glancing up, she noticed G wasn't behind the counter. A young, teenaged girl with a nose ring looked at her. "Cappuccino?" Audrey said.

Then she pulled out her phone, looking for any information from Orlando Falco as to how the vote had gone. It was still too early. The meeting likely wasn't until this afternoon. So she texted Brina: *Help. I need you to talk me down from the ledge.*

A moment later, Brina came back with: *Oh, look. The prodigal sister.*

Audrey rolled her eyes. What had it been, two days since she'd last texted her? *Sorry. Been busy. But really. I'm at a crossroads. M came by last night. Brought me dinner.*

Seconds later: *!!!!! DETAILS.*

She sighed, thinking of it. She'd given him wine, they'd shared a few flirts, and then… he'd run off like a bat out of hell. Typical day in

Audrey's romantic life. Brina probably would've had him professing his undying love by now.

She typed in: *We just talked. He helped me sand my floors.*

Even Audrey had to wince at how lame that sounded.

I'm almost ashamed to be related to you, girl. So… while he was sanding your floors, did you snap any pics?

Of course Brina would be concerned about that. Brina would probably have a catalogue of all his body parts by now. *No.*

Her sister sent over a rolling-eyes emoticon. *So what's the problem?*

Audrey's fingers flew over the keyboard, then hovered over the send button. She read the words again and again, hardly able to believe she was going to admit this. *I think I have a crush on abs.*

Brina sent the emoticon of clapping hands. *Of course you do. But at least you're finally admitting it now.*

She looked up to find the waitress staring at her, expectant, coffee pot in hand. Audrey dragged the tiny cup closer and inhaled the scent of strong brew. "Oh. Um. Brioche? Um …" That was really the only thing she knew that Sicilians ate for breakfast. She grabbed the menu and pointed to something that sounded nice.

The girl came back with a tiny plate, covered in a doily. On it, what looked like a sugar donut.

Audrey took a bite, then gobbled the rest of it down in a flash. Did G make that? Wow. Why was it that all the men she knew in Sicily were not only good-looking, but good cooks, as well? She pointed to her plate, mouth still full. "Another?"

The girl set another one down on her plate.

"Grazie."

"That's one thing I'm going to miss. The *ciambella,"* a voice with a Brooklyn accent said behind her. She spun on her stool to see the American expat she'd met a week or so ago. He patted his hefty stomach. "But my stomach will probably be better off without it."

"Hi …" she said, trying to recall his name. "Bruno?"

He nodded. "That's right. Good to see you again."

He was wearing a black leather jacket, his New York Giants cap turned backward, and jeans. His duffel was on the ground next to him. "You're going back to the States, huh?"

"Yep. Plane leaves in a couple hours. Just waiting on my ride."

She grabbed a napkin and wiped the sugar from her chin. "And how did the house hunting go? When do you think you're coming back?"

His lips twisted, and he hitched both shoulders. "I got to say, never. Unfortunately. I'm actually cutting the trip short, it went so bad. Guess the dollar house dream was just that—a dream."

"What? What happened? You seemed so excited about the possibility before. Didn't you find any good properties?"

"No, I found plenty. And my girl, she was really hyped on coming out here and being with me." He glanced around, as if he was afraid someone else might be listening. Then he leaned in and whispered, "I don't think this place is very welcoming."

Audrey's eyes widened.

He chuckled sadly. "Yeah. I know. Me, coming from New York, not thinking the place is very welcoming. But it's true. These locals can give New Yorkers a bad name. How do you put up with it?"

"Well, I... I haven't really noticed it, except—"

"I guess even if you did, you're SOL, having bought the place sight unseen, huh?" He motioned to the waitress with his credit card and bill. She came over to take it.

"Well, no. Actually, people haven't been that bad. Most have been very nice. At least, so far. What have you been noticing? The locals have been mean to you?"

"Not all the locals. One in particular. Some councilwoman. My Realtor came by one day and told me she was giving all this trouble to anyone outside of the country."

"You mean Mimi Catalano?"

He nodded. "That's her. She might've died, but her ghost is still haunting this place. She has a lot of supporters. They're the ones trying to run us locals out of town. I can't believe you haven't felt the pressure."

"Oh, I have," Audrey mumbled, thinking of the council meeting that would decide her fate in this town. It was sad that Bruno's fate had already been decided. It seemed premature. "Sure, some locals might be bullies, but as more and more expats move in, it'll be more friendly to people like us. Especially when they see how necessary we are to their economy. Are you sure you won't stay? At least, try?"

He shook his head. "Sorry. But if things continue this way, and the council keeps giving us expats a nudge out the door, the one-dollar house program's going to fail. That's all there is to it."

Audrey's stomach turned. She'd never really thought about that. Oh, she was worried that her business could fail, and that she might not have the money to do the reno, but she always thought Mussomeli would grow, with or without her, into a vibrant, exciting city. The thought of foreigners escaping the dying remains of town... of the houses crumbling even more... of more sick, hungry strays roaming the streets... It filled her with dread.

"I'm sorry you're leaving, Bruno," she said.

He grabbed his credit card back from the waitress and peered out the window. "I am, too. There's my cab. Nice chatting with you. Good luck," he said, grabbing his duffel and heading out, as Audrey finished in her head: *I'm going to need it.*

She watched him leave and dropped her half-eaten pastry to her plate, appetite gone. On the curb, the driver opened the trunk, letting Bruno shove his big luggage inside. He opened the door, pulling his long, beefy limbs into the car, scanning the area as if he was hoping to avoid someone.

Suddenly, something occurred to her. Something that Nessa had said. *He was tall. Big. He was wearing like a hat, I think.*

"*Principessa!*" a voice called from the back room, behind the counter, but Audrey was only vaguely aware of it. She was too busy thinking of Nessa's description. Before, she'd thought it worthless, but now, everything seemed to fall into place.

Tall. Big and bulky. Wearing a hat.

"Oh my God," Audrey whispered aloud, rising slowly from her seat.

Grabbing her phone and shoving it into her pocket, she rushed for the exit.

CHAPTER TWENTY TWO

Audrey bolted for the door, swerving around customers. She threw it open and exploded out onto the narrow street, but by the time she got there, breathing hard, the taxi was already gone.

I got this, she told herself, breaking into a run, heading down the road the way the cab must've gone.

All of the roads around the area were very narrow and one-way, so she reasoned that in order to get onto the main road, headed toward the airport in Palermo, they'd have to get onto *Via Barcellona.*

Hanging a quick right, she dodged into an alley. The stench of garbage nearly overpowered her. Pumping her legs, trying not to pay attention to the burning in her lungs, she ran until she came to a fence. At first, she thought she was stuck, but then she spotted an opening in it. She slipped through and kept going, the walls of the buildings blurring around her.

She tore into someone's small patch of backyard, into their freshly washed laundry, dripping from a crooked line. Pushing it out of the way, she came to a short chain-link fence. She climbed over it, hurdling over an old manual lawnmower before her ankle got caught in a coil of watering hose. Finally, she extricated herself and raced down a narrow passage between two homes. When she cleared the houses, she raced between two cars, into the street.

The horn blared. Tires screeched. She took one look to the left and her mouth formed the shape of a scream as the taxi bore down on her, and one thought filled her head: *Maybe I don't got this.*

Before she could let out the shriek in her throat, the cab came to a complete stop, its front bumper just inches from her kneecaps.

She threw her hands down on the hood of the car. "Wait! Wait right there!" she warned the driver.

Bruno was already opening the door, pulling his hefty body from the seat, a bewildered expression on his face. "What the—"

He looked as though he was about to ask her if she was okay, but she didn't need the sympathy of a murderer. Gathering every last bit of breath into her lungs, she pointed an accusing finger at him. "It was you, wasn't it?" she shouted. "Wasn't it?"

He stared at her, squinting slightly. "Me, what?"

"You're tall …" She heaved a big breath. "Big…" She gasped.

He leaned in close to her. "Are you okay?"

She ignored him, still panting and waving a hand in front of her face. "Yeah. Fine. You're wearing a hat …" She trailed off when she realized just what she'd said to Nessa earlier. *And so are half the men in town.*

He scowled. "And?"

She kept her eyes on him, though she was aware of other people on the sidewalks, stopping, watching the scene. "And… you killed her. Mimi." She raised her chin, daring him to defy her.

"Who the hell is Mimi?"

"The councilwoman …" she started, still indignant, though her righteous armor was beginning to show chinks. "Obviously. You should know. You killed her. On that beach?"

He laughed. Long and hard, no holds barred. "What beach? Who do you think you are? Agatha Christie? I didn't kill no one. I've never been to any beach in my life, especially around here. I don't like sand."

"You're lying. I can see it in your eyes. You must've. Maybe you followed her."

He laughed. "You really think I'd waste my time going all the way down there, just to kill that councilwoman?"

Her eyes widened. "You must've been. Otherwise, how would you know how steep the walk is?"

He froze, and his face began to turn red, just like Nessa's had when she'd been caught in a lie.

Oh, my god, she thought. *I've got him! I am turning out to be a regular Miss Marple!*

Emboldened, she continued: "You were walking on the beach and you saw her, you took your chance, and you shoved her. You killed her, and then you ran away. And now you're running away before you get caught. Admit it. I know someone who was running on the beach. She saw you. She can identify you."

More people were now gathering around, coming out of local businesses and homes. There was an Italian butcher's shop, full of meats and sausages hanging in the window, that Audrey had never seen before, but must be a pretty happening place, judging from how many people poured out of it to see what was going on.

But Bruno did not admit anything. He crossed his arms. "I'm not saying another word. I'm getting in my taxi and going to the airport. So get out of the road and let me go."

Bruno tried to go back to his seat, but Audrey stood firm, in front of the taxi's hood.

He gritted his teeth. "Hey. Scram. You're going to make me miss my flight."

She shrugged innocently, then smiled as the sound of sirens filled the air. A police car appeared in the road, behind the cab, heading toward the small crowd. "All right. If you won't tell me, then maybe you will tell the police?"

Bruno looked over his shoulder, threw up his hands, and muttered a torrent of curses any sailor would've been impressed by.

The police car slowed to a stop behind the cab, and to Audrey's delight, Officer Ricci, her old friend, stepped out. He'd been in charge of monitoring her house twenty-four-seven when she was suspected of murdering the foreman, and he'd eaten a healthy dose of crow after she was cleared. She and the young, baby-faced officer were friends now.

"Audrey?" he asked, as if he wasn't particularly surprised to see her here.

"Hi, Officer Ricci," she called, waving to him. "This here is Bruno. He is trying to leave the country for good, without explaining to you why he was on the same beach as Mimi Catalano on the morning she was killed."

A collective gasp rose up from the crowd.

Officer Ricci approached, his suspicion misplaced. He was doubtfully eyeing her, instead of the culprit, even though she was pointing at him with both hands.

"Audrey. How do you get to be part of this?" he asked in very fragmented English, staring her down like she was a recalcitrant child.

"I just—" That was a long story, one she didn't want to tell, when they were so close to cracking the darn case. "It's not important. What's important is that this man was on the beach when—"

Ricci held up a hand. "I get it. *Grazie.*" He finally looked at Bruno. "Is it true you were leaving town?"

Bruno's eyes went to the sky. "Yes." He checked his phone. "Probably not now. I'm gonna miss my flight."

"American? What's your name?"

"Bruno Altavera." He reached into the pocket of his leather jacket and pulled out his passport, opening it to the front page. "See?"

Officer Ricci took the passport and read it, writing something down in a small, spiral notepad. "And is what she say true? You saw the victim that morning?"

He dragged in a breath and looked at Audrey. "Yeah. I did."

More gasps in the crowd.

But before Audrey could feel vindicated for her crazy behavior, he shouted, "But I didn't kill her! I swear. Yes, I saw her there. I was down there fishing. I like to fish, but nothing was biting, so I was pissed. She started telling me I wasn't welcome here, whatever." He shrugged. "So I might've told her a couple of inappropriate things in the heat of the moment. But that was it. Then I just gathered up my stuff and left."

"Did you shove the victim?"

"No. No, I didn't lay a finger on her. I was too far away. She was walking in the loose sand and I was down by the water. We just kind of yelled at each other. And then we went our separate ways. I went back up to town, and she kept walking the beach, which I thought was dumb, considering she was wearing those stupid red heels. But I didn't kill her. Didn't touch her."

Ricci kept scribbling something. "You no can leave. Not until we sort this out. You understand?"

"But I've got a ticket! I have a flight! I have a life to get back to. You can't keep me here."

Audrey rolled her eyes. She knew all too well. *Yes, they can. And they will.*

The cab driver, a spry old man, had jumped out of the cab and deposited Bruno's bag at his feet, muttering something in Italian that sounded like *Crazy Americans*. Popping back behind his seat, he stared daggers at Bruno, his knuckles wrapped tight around the steering wheel. He revved the engine and inched closer to them, as if he was ready to take off the moment that they moved out of the way. Officer Ricci took Audrey's sleeve, pulled her aside, and motioned to the driver to continue on.

The driver floored it, tires squealing as it peeled around a sharp corner.

Officer Ricci turned to Bruno, whose face was so red, he looked like a bowl of tomato soup, a pressure cooker ready to explode. "*Signore*, where are you staying?"

He was still scowling at Audrey. "This is B.S. You're going to hear from my attorney." Then he let out a dramatic sigh, and his voice softened. "The Regalpetra. On *Via Garibaldi*."

"*Grazie, signore,*" the officer said, writing that down. He turned to Audrey. "Come. I walk you home."

"I'm actually going to the clinic."

"I walk you to the clinic, then."

She nodded. "Thank you."

Truthfully, she didn't want to go anywhere alone right now. Especially with the way Bruno, a suspected murderer she'd just accused, was looking at her.

CHAPTER TWENTY THREE

When Officer Ricci brought her to the clinic, it was after nine. Audrey was frantic, expecting her first appointment would be waiting outside, impatient. But as she approached, she saw no one. Then she realized that the door sign had been flipped to *APERTO*, and the door itself was a bit open. There were even lights on inside.

"I'm sure I closed up yesterday. What is going on?" she wondered aloud, running ahead the next few steps. Had someone broken in?

Ricci caught up with her and grabbed her arm. "Hold on. Let me check."

Before he could, though, she spied Mason through the storefront window, straightening some of the magazines. Her nine o'clock was sitting in the waiting room with her pooch, patiently reading a magazine.

"It's okay," she told the officer. "I can take it from here."

"You sure?"

She nodded and thanked him.

"All right," Ricci said. "You call me if you need anything."

She jogged inside. Mason grinned at her. "You must've been really tired last night. You forgot to lock up."

Thoughts of the text she'd sent Brina shortly before her adventure swirled in her head, and her face heated. "Oh. I did?"

"Yeah. So when I got here, your nine was standing outside. I thought, no sense in letting her wait, so I let her in. Hope you don't mind." He stared closely at her, as if he could read that text she'd sent Brina right on her face. "Everything okay? Why are you red?"

She touched her cheek. "Nothing. No, I don't mind. Thank you. I was—" She stopped short before telling him about her jaunt down the street, after the potential murderer. It was too long a story for now. "Great."

Audrey tried to skirt away from him, head down, wondering if she'd always feel like a lovesick teenager when it came to men she liked. Why couldn't she act like a normal adult and chill?

Mason said, "I took care of the animals and got the exam room ready, so you should be all set."

She spun and stared at him for a moment. Who was this man and what had he done with the old Mason? "Are *you* okay?"

"Yeah. Why?"

"You told me you hated the animals. And you took care of them?"

"Yep."

This would be, in the Hallmark Christmas movies, where he clasped his hands together and professed his love for her. *I did it because I realized how much I adore you.* But it wasn't Christmas, and she wasn't that lucky.

She peered behind the counter, toward the kennels, wondering if all was okay. There were no strange sounds coming from there, just a lot of normal yips and the scrabbling of little paws on the floor. "And no problems?"

"Not one."

Just then, her nine o'clock appointment shifted in her chair. It wasn't an act of impatience, but it jarred Audrey out of her silly romantic thoughts. Besides, Mason was starting to look at her like she had something coming out of her nose. *Focus, Audrey.*

"Ohhhkay," she said suspiciously, then checked the appointment book and turned to the woman with a bright smile. "Hello, is this Marco? What a beautiful dog you are! Come on back."

Everything went like clockwork with the next patient. She went through the Abruzzese Sheepdog's check-up, and when she was finishing up with him, she came outside to find that Mason had disappeared. She checked Marco's owner out herself and said goodbye, and suddenly heard an excited barking coming from the play area by the dog kennel. She walked into the back to find Mason playing with Polpetto, the mastiff jumping up and down like a little puppy as Mason held a ball for him. Mason had a big smile on his face that she'd never seen before, and it made him look even more breathtaking.

"What are you doing?" she asked, flabbergasted.

"I was just… playing fetch with the dog." He gave her a nonchalant shrug and dropped the ball on the ground, this time not complaining at all that his hand was wet with drool. "Need help with something else?"

"What are you, sick?" She thought about feeling his forehead, but that would require touching him, something that gave her excited tingles she wasn't sure she should be feeling.

He shrugged. "Just trying to be helpful."

"If you don't mind… it would be amazing if you could take Polpetto for a walk. He's used to going on them. Actually, all the dogs could use exercise, and I have a full list of appointments all morning."

"No problem," he said, swiping a leash off the counter. "Hey. You gonna tell me why you were late? And had a cop drop you off? And why your pants are like that?"

She looked down. Her favorite jeans had a tear down the thigh, likely one she'd sustained while hurdling over one of the chain-link fences during her hot pursuit. She touched it. It wasn't bleeding, at least, but unless she could find a giant patch, the jeans were ruined.

"Ugh. Great." She sighed. "I thought I found Mimi Catalano's murderer. Chased him down the street."

He leaned forward on the counter, interested. "*You* did? Let me guess. He got away."

"No. I caught him. Actually. His taxi nearly caught me and flattened me like a little pancake." She shrugged. "The police came and questioned him but he denied everything. Only thing was, Nessa saw him on the beach. He said he was there, but he didn't murder anyone."

"That's interesting. How did you suspect him?"

"Nessa said she saw a big guy with a hat. And he told me he was getting trouble from the local council. He was an American, so I figured he was getting the same treatment you and I were getting, from Mimi. Considering he was at the beach at the time… it all fits together. Only thing is …"

"He says he's innocent."

"Yeah. But don't they all? I caught him trying to skip town early. It just makes sense. Maybe the police will question him more, and he'll crack. Still …" She frowned. "Something doesn't sit right with me. I mean, he ticks off all the boxes, and yet… I feel like something is off."

"Right… probably the fact that you chased down and accused of murder a *big* guy that probably could've flattened you. Boston, you need to stop taking chances like that, don't you think?"

She was about to argue, but she'd seen that rabid look in Bruno's eyes. If the police hadn't shown up, it could've been bad for her. "Yes. I guess you are right. I'll be more careful." She gnawed on her lip. "But that might just be the New York in him. There's plenty of people who get emotional about things. Doesn't make them killers. I don't know. It's so confusing."

"You don't need to know. Leave it to the police, all right? All you need to do is take care of these animals," he reminded her. Polpetto had been standing beside him, gazing up at him like an adoring fan. Mason clipped the leash on his collar. "I guess you won't get into too much trouble if I leave you alone here?"

She fisted her hands on her hips. Way to talk to her like a child. But she'd earned that by acting like one without any concern for her own safety. "I'll be fine. Go."

When he left, she sat down at the reception desk to try to go over some of the financials and balance the books. She opened the Excel file and her head spun when she saw the number in red. It was a small number, really, but one that was likely to grow if that tax went through.

The phone rang. Maybe this was serendipity. *Oh, please let that be Orlando Falco, telling me the stray tax is off the table!*

She answered with her usual, "Dr. Smart Veterinary Clinic, how may I help you?"

"Hello," a female voice said, with a European accent Audrey couldn't place. "I saw your flyer."

"Yes. Great. Do you have any information about the dog we found?"

"No, not that dog. But I was wondering. Did you happen to find any other stray dogs? I'm missing my Pepe. He's a white poodle."

"Oh. No. I'm sorry. How long has he been missing?"

"Since Tuesday."

Tuesday. The day she found Polpetto on the beach. The day Mimi Catalano was murdered. Lots of strange things happened that day, hadn't they?

"We don't have an animal of that description, but I can take your information, and if he comes in here, I can let you know."

"That would be wonderful," the woman said, and gave her address, one that wasn't at all familiar to Audrey.

"Thank you. Where in Mussomeli is that?" Audrey asked.

"It's outside the city. On *Lago Sfendato*."

Something prickled on the back of Audrey's neck. *Lago Sfendato*. The same place where Mimi Catalano's body was found. Lots of strange things had happened *on that beach*, on that day. "And how did you think you lost him?"

"It's odd. We always keep him in a fenced yard. Someone must've opened the back gate. Pepe couldn't reach the latch on his own. We're so sad without him."

"Thank you. I'll keep an eye out," she said.

The phone rang again as soon as she hung up. She answered once again, now less hopeful that it would be Orlando, telling her the tax troubles were over.

A voice began to rush mile-a-minute in Italian. She brought up Google translate on the computer, but the only word she could put in was *il negozio*, which meant "store." That, and the speaker, a deep male voice, said something about a *cane*, which she'd learned was Italian for dog.

"Mi dispiace, ma non parlo bene l'italiano," she said in her terrible, broken accent. At least that little guidebook had been good for something. "You say you were at the store? And you saw the flyer about the found dog? Do you have information about it?"

"Si. Yes. I do."

Thank goodness, the man spoke English. Hope igniting in her, she grabbed a pen and paper from the desk and said, "Do you know who the owner is?"

"Yes," the man said. "It's me. I'm the owner. That's my big boy, Tito."

"Oh! Wonderful," Audrey gushed excitedly. "Well, we've been keeping him here at the clinic, taking care of him. He sure is a busy boy who likes his walks. He didn't have a collar at the time so we didn't know his name."

"Ah. Well, I am so grateful you found him. I have missed him very much. He's like a son to me."

She smiled. She loved dog owners like that, who considered their pets part of the family, and could only imagine the heartache and worry he'd been going through. "Your name?"

"Alberto. Alberto Nucci."

"Well, Mr. Nucci. He's here at the clinic on *Via Barcellona.* The address was on the flyer. Would you like to come and pick him up?"

"Yes. I'll be there right away. Thank you, thank you again."

He ended the call, and she squealed excitedly. Polpetto would be so happy. He'd go back to his forever home, with his loving owner. How wonderful.

But the more she thought about it, sadness began to descend upon her. Her little Polpetto, the good dog, would be gone for good. She pushed those thoughts away. *Audrey, you always get so wrapped up in your patients' lives. You need to stop that right now.*

She stood up to greet her next patient, who had just arrived. It didn't matter what she felt. If everything worked out, and it looked like it was going to, Polpetto would be so thrilled to be back in his loving home, and that was the most important thing of all.

CHAPTER TWENTY FOUR

"Ciao! Mettiti in sesto presto!" Audrey called to the ailing dog as she helped him and his owner out to the sidewalk. Those words, the Italian form of "get well soon," were some of the few she'd already learned, out of necessity's sake. The little dog gave her sad but grateful eyes. Poor thing had a bit of a stomachache. Nothing serious, but he was clearly not his best self.

When she went back inside, she found Polpetto back in the kennel, and the stray pit bull cross was gone. So Mason was really working through the strays, making sure all of them were getting their walks? Great. He'd also left her a message: *The dog smelled. Gave him a bath, too.*

Her jaw dropped. If she didn't know better, she'd think Mason was angling for a raise. That was, if she'd even been paying him to begin with.

So what was his angle?

Polpetto yipped excitedly when she appeared in the doorway and wagged his sharp, lethal weapon of a tail. "Wanting another walk so soon, boy? You were spoiled by your owner, weren't you?" she said, going over and rubbing his brindle coat. It was still damp from the bath and smelled lightly of soap. He stared up at her with those typical sad mastiff eyes. "But I have good news for you."

He panted, handing her his paw again.

She crouched in front of him. "Yes. That's right. Your owner is on his way to see you, right this minute!"

His panting sped up and he looked past her, toward the door, almost as if he understood exactly what she was saying to him.

"I'll miss you, though, buddy. Promise me you'll come by to see me now and then ..." She sighed. "All right, *Tito*?"

He barked in answer.

She left him in the kennel and went out to the front of the clinic. She sat down and took a deep breath for the second time that day. Pure bliss. She could get used to having her days like this. Just as she was about to dig back into the financials, the door opened, and a man with a knit skip cap and North Face jacket came in. He was so tall, he had to duck his head not to hit the transom.

Audrey stared at him, a feeling of déjà vu hitting her as he approached the reception desk. "Hello," he said, giving her a tentative smile as his eyes volleyed around the reception area.

"Can I help you?" she asked.

When he removed his cap to reveal a bald head, the pieces of the puzzle came together.

Of course. Mr. Clean, from the council meeting. He was the guy who'd gone off on Mimi Catalano. His face had been a lot redder, then, twisted in anger. Now, he looked normal. Relaxed. Calm.

He said, "Alberto Nucci."

She stared at him, as the pieces continued to fall into place. He knew Mimi Catalano. He'd hated her. He had a temper.

She realized she hadn't yet responded to him when he continued, "You have my Tito?"

"Oh! Yes. I do. It's so nice to have found you," she blurted, shaking her head. "We found him running along the beach. You take that route often on your walks? He seemed to know it pretty well."

"Yes," the man said. "That's Tito's favorite walk. He loves to splash in the lake. We go walking there twice a day."

"You must be very fit. Those stairs are a killer."

"No, no," he said, shaking his head. "I live down on the lake. I have a house there, overlooking the water."

"You… do?" she spit out, the gears in her head starting to churn.

"Yes. I thought he was in our yard, but he must've somehow gotten out. The gate was wide open. He's never done that before."

"He hasn't?" she asked, an all-over cold falling over her body, casting it in millions of goosebumps. That woman who'd called before lived on the lake, and had also had her gate open. She'd lost her dog just the same way. There was no secret that Mimi was no friend to animals. Maybe… was it possible that Mimi had had something to do with all of this?

She must've waited a beat too long, because Alberto's smile faded. "Are you going to show me my dog?"

"Oh." She jumped out of her seat and went around the reception desk. "Of course. Yes. Right this way. He's just had a bath and everything."

She led him down the hallway in a daze. *I need to call DiNardo. Someone needs to question this guy.*

When she got to the kennel, Tito began to wag his tail excitedly. He let out a loud, happy bark. The second Audrey opened the door, the dog raced for his owner, jumping up on him and panting with excitement. "Hey, boy. It's good to see you."

Suddenly, an idea popped into her head. "I'll let you two get reacquainted while I go and put together the paperwork you have to fill out."

He twisted his head toward her. "Paperwork? What kind of paperwork?"

"Oh. Just routine forms," she answered vaguely. To be honest, there was no paperwork. But if it would stall him from leaving while DiNardo came over, it would be worth it.

She rushed to the reception desk and quickly dialed his number. When he answered, she cupped her hand around her mouth and said, "It's Audrey. I need you at the clinic," in a low voice.

"Hello? Who is this?"

She rolled her eyes. "Clinic. Now!"

"Audrey?"

"Yes. Are you—"

"It's lunch, and I'm just sitting down to—"

"NOW," she barked, quickly hanging up as she heard Tito's paws scrabbling on the floor behind her.

She looked up just as Alberto walked the dog out, now wearing the red collar, which she'd left in the room, in a bin with a bunch of other collars. "I'm glad you found his collar," he told her.

"Yes, well, actually, he did …" she said, becoming more convinced by the second that she was looking into the eyes of the man who'd murdered Mimi Catalano. How had he known Tito had lost his collar? Why hadn't he just assumed she'd taken it off to have the bath? "He found it on the beach …"

"Did he, now?" He beamed down at his dog. Then he looked up at her. "Paperwork?"

"Right, um …" She reached into a file folder and rifled through all the papers. Adoption forms, receipts, surveys, foster care questionnaires. "Geez. I thought it was here. I think I have to go print out some more copies. It'll only be a moment."

She shook her mouse to wake up her computer, and he crossed his arms impatiently.

"You know," she said conversationally, willing her heart to stop beating like it was trying to escape her chest. "I thought you looked familiar. I just realized where I knew you from."

He studied her, silently stroking Tito's ears. Though her eyes were focused on the computer screen, she could tell from the way he tapped his foot that he had no interest.

"The council meeting!" she said, still moving her mouse aimlessly through various folders. "You were the one who got up and really ripped Mimi Catalano a new one about her stray tax. Weren't you?"

She glanced at him, and he visibly stiffened. His voice was low. "I did not get along with that woman."

"I could tell that." She swallowed, wondering how much longer she'd have to stall him for. Venturing a glance out the window, she finally opened a document, then sighed. "Wrong one."

She closed the document, and the man fidgeted from foot to foot. "Is this going to take much longer? I have someplace to be."

She closed the document. "Not much! Unfortunately, there are rules, and I have to have all my i's dotted and t's crossed. You understand."

But the more he stood there, the more she could tell that he didn't understand, and that he was not only getting upset... he was getting suspicious of her stalling tactics. That original reddish tone began to spread under his cheeks, catching like a forest fire.

"Oh! It might be in here," she said, opening another file as she furtively glanced out the window. Where was DiNardo? He'd done this before to her, at the lumber yard, and she probably would've been killed if it weren't for Nick. But Nick was nowhere in sight, nor was Mason, or that slow-poke DiNardo. He hadn't actually said he was on his way. What if he'd ignored her? What if he'd completely forced Audrey's plea for help from his mind and was sitting down to a nice plate of pasta for lunch, right now?

"I've had enough," he said, his voice low and menacing. "I'll give you my address. You find he forms and get back to me. Okay?"

"No! No, I can't do that. Legal regulations demand that I—"

"Listen, Doctor." She turned to him. His face was lit up, ready to blow like a volcano. She sunk back in her chair as he towered over her. "I don't know what kind of game you're playing, but I've had enough."

CHAPTER TWENTY FIVE

"I'm sorry," Audrey squeaked, unable to find more of her voice. She pointed to the computer. "The clinic is new, and my filing system is clearly a mess."

She giggled to mask the fear that was gripping her.

His frown deepened. "Yeah. It is."

"But I really do need you to fill out these forms," she added, trying on her most charming smile.

That didn't work either. He leaned closer, his breath sour on her face. Then he nudged the back of her chair. "Fine. Find them. But if you don't in sixty seconds, I'm out of here."

"Okay!" she said, scooting the wheeled chair closer to the computer. He backed away and started to look at a neutering display. Sensing his owner's unease, Tito lay on the floor, being an extra good boy. She managed another quick glance out the storefront window.

Eureka. DiNardo was there, walking purposefully for the door.

Audrey jumped from her seat and ran for it. "One moment!" she called over her shoulder, rushing for the exit, opening the door just as he was about to come inside.

"Audrey. What was that call all ab—"

Before he could finish, she nudged the detective out onto the street, as he gave her a look she'd come to be accustomed to. It was the *What on earth do you think you're up to?* look. She knew it very well.

"It's him," she whispered, shivering even in the warmth of the early afternoon sun. "I know it is."

"It's... who, exactly?"

"The killer!" she whispered. "The person who murdered Mimi Catalano. Who else?"

Scratching his head, he craned his neck to peer in the storefront window. "Yeah, um... Audrey? Let's not jump to conclusions, shall we?"

"I'm not jumping to conclusions! He's really here!" She almost jumped up and down and stomped her feet, but she doubted that would help her case. At least they had him trapped. He couldn't go anywhere, unless he wanted to rush past DiNardo. And DiNardo was packing heat.

At least, she thought so. There was a suspicious bulge under his jacket, near his chest, that she figured was a gun. "I'm sure of it."

"Officer Ricci said you sounded pretty sure of yourself this morning, when you nearly tackled that American in the street."

Audrey winced. So he'd heard about that?

"What were you thinking?" he demanded, crossing his arms in front of him. "Did that scene at the lumber yard teach you nothing?"

"All right. I know I've behaved recklessly in the past. But I didn't this time. I called you to intercede, didn't I?" She gave him her most innocent look. "So do what you have to do. Question him. That's all I'm asking."

"Fine." He reached into his pocket. "What did you say this guy's name was?"

"Alberto Nucci. He lives by the lake. The stray dog I found was his. He was at a council meeting before Mimi Catalano was killed, and he made no secret of the fact that he hated her guts!" Audrey exclaimed excitedly. "I have a feeling that Mimi Catalano was down by the lake, letting dogs out of their backyards so that she could prove the stray problem was too big a problem for me to handle and encourage euthanasia. He probably caught her. He has tons of motive, and I bet he doesn't have an alibi."

He held up both hands. "Don't get carried away. That's only your theory. Where's the proof?"

"Do I have to do everything for you?" She shook her head. "But I do have proof. Remember that collar I found? I had it off the dog because we'd just given him a bath, so it was just sitting on the counter. When he put it on the dog, he said, *Thanks for finding the collar.* Now, how would he know that the collar was missing if he wasn't on the beach the day she was killed?"

He shrugged. "I don't know. Maybe he lost the collar before that? But it doesn't matter, Audrey. It'll still be your word against his."

"So you're not going to question him?"

"I am," he said, reaching for the door. Before he opened it, he turned back to her. "But I want you to promise me you'll stay out of it. *Capisci?*"

She nodded. If she had to.

He went inside and stopped short in the doorway. She peered over his shoulder and saw the problem before DiNardo even said, "Now, where is he?"

She pushed him aside and looked around the reception area. Then she rushed into the back, searching through all the rooms, bewildered. "I don't know! Where could he have—"

She stopped when DiNardo pointed down the corridor. There was a dark staircase that she had yet to travel down because it looked like it descended into hell. "Back door?" he asked.

Of course. Was she stupid? Just because she ignored it didn't mean it didn't exist.

Skipping into a run, Audrey rushed down the stairs. Sure enough, they ended at an old wooden door that was now hanging partially ajar. She threw it open and burst out into a narrow alley that backed up to a solid wood fence. Looking up and down the path, she let out a curse.

"Back door," she grumbled, thumping the front of her skull with the heel of her hand.

She was just about to go back inside when she squinted down the alley and saw a familiar apricot-colored blur in the distance.

"Polpetto?" she called. "Is that you, boy?"

He let out one very sharp bark and turned in a circle.

She knew what that bark meant. She'd heard it on the beach, when she'd first met him and found Mimi's body. It was a simple command: *Follow me.*

"He wants us to go with him," she shouted, breaking into a run.

By the time she got to the corner, she already had a stitch in her side, but the sound of DiNardo's footsteps right behind her spurred her on. When she got to the T where the alley met the street, she swung her head around.

Sure enough, Alberto was rushing down the street, his dog on his heels.

Sucking in a breath and letting it out, she started to run again. Unfortunately, uphill. This time, DiNardo easily overtook her, crossing a side street as a car slammed on its brakes, narrowly missing him. The driver honked its horn and started to proceed again, just as Audrey flew into the intersection, placing her hands on the hood to avoid being hit for the second time that day.

The man was fast. He might not have climbed those stairs to the beach, but he was definitely fitter than Audrey. Fitter than DiNardo, too, because it was clear he was widening the gap. She could barely see the Polpetto beyond DiNardo, who was pumping his arms and legs with all his might.

Just when she was about to give up, she heard a cry up ahead. It was a man, but it sounded decidedly... girlish.

Polpetto had pinned his owner to the ground, and was now standing on his back, licking his face playfully.

DiNardo came to a quick stop, with Audrey right behind him. Audrey smiled. "I bet next time you'll think before you say a dog's not important, huh?"

CHAPTER TWENTY SIX

In a surprising display of force, Detective DiNardo yanked Alberto Nucci from the sidewalk by his collar and shoved him up against the side of the building, shouting something in Italian. Nucci, beaten, nodded and held up his hands. Audrey tried to follow their conversation, but she was lost after she heard the name *Tito* a couple times.

"What is he saying?" Audrey demanded. "Is he denying it, the scoundrel?"

"No," DiNardo said, loosening his grip on the man's shirt. "He says that Mimi Catalano was in the habit of going along that route, opening gates, removing collars, to make the stray problem look worse than it was."

"Ah-ha! I told you," Audrey said proudly. "And? Then what happened?"

DiNardo looked at Alberto, whose face was red from exertion, that blue vein at his temple popping in the sunlight like it was about to burst.

"She's a snake. A vicious snake, and not just to newcomers. I caught her doing it. I was having breakfast that morning and saw her at my back gate. Tito, he likes everyone. Even *streghe*."

Audrey lifted a brow in confusion. *"Streghe?"*

"Witches," DiNardo explained.

The man nodded. "Right. I saw her taking the collar from his neck, and then she ran off with it. Wearing heels, *stupida*. I caught up with her on the beach, after she'd gotten rid of the collar somewhere, and I demanded she tell me what she did."

"And you fought?"

"No. Well, yes. But with words. I never touched her. I wouldn't have. There were other people on the beach at the time. A jogger ...a fisherman. I didn't want to make a scene. I wanted her to tell me where the collar was and admit what she'd been doing."

"Did she?"

"No, she was a stubborn one. She denied everything. She told me it was my word against hers, and that I'd pay for attempting to humiliate her in that meeting. The she turned away from me and lost her balance.

I went to help her up and… she wasn't moving. There was so much blood." He shook his head, clearly perturbed by the memory.

Audrey eyed the man skeptically. The man she'd seen, with the red face and the pulsing vein, had a temper. This version sounded far too innocent. "Do you believe that, Detective?"

"Doesn't matter what I believe. It's for the court to decide."

Nucci hung his head. "It's the truth. I shouldn't have run off, but I wasn't thinking. It was an accident."

Detective DiNardo reached under his jacket and pulled out a pair of handcuffs. "All right. I think you and I need to have a talk downtown."

He twisted him around and snapped the cuffs on. Audrey hugged herself, thinking. It might not have been quite as innocent as Nucci had said, but even so, it was a sobering reminder that life was precious. She had to feel sorry for Mimi Catalano. Even though she'd made life difficult for people, she hadn't deserved to die. No one did.

As the detective spoke to Alberto, possibly reading him his rights, Mason came jogging up the street with one of the strays on a leash. "What's going on?" he asked her, then took notice of DiNardo and the cuffed man. "Wait. Don't tell me …"

She shrugged. "You missed all the fun."

"Looks like I did. Did that guy—"

"Yep. He said it was an accident, but who knows? Polpetto's owner, like I always suspected."

Mason nodded. "Yes. You did. You're good, girl. Maybe you went into the wrong line of work."

She laughed and looked at him. "Maybe I did. But I still didn't solve the biggest mystery of all. Which is why you've been acting so suspicious lately. Is it because of your mysterious guest?"

"Partly." He scratched the back of his head sheepishly. "Fine. I'll tell you. My finances might not have been as flush as I was hoping, recently."

She stared at him. He'd said before his family had money. Lots of it. Gorgeous, handy, and loaded… as if he needed anything to make him more of a catch. He'd moved out here without any expectation of working at all once he set up his place—just living a simple Mediterranean bachelor lifestyle. "I thought you said …"

"I know what I said. I was wrong. Let's just say that my gravy train's gone off the rails. Anyway, I've been working down the street, stocking shelves at the market overnight. So… I'm sorry if I've been falling asleep at times. It's not you."

"Oh …" she said. Well, obviously. That made sense. More sense than him partying it up at clubs in town or getting into shady business. He didn't seem like that kind of person at all. She clasped a hand over her mouth. "And you drove me to the lake when you should've been sleeping, that time? You've been coming right from that job to work for me?"

He nodded.

Her heart melted. So what did that mean, for her? Did that mean he …

She didn't want to think about it, because if it did, she'd start giggling like a moron again. She clasped a hand over her mouth to stifle whatever weird sounds might come out. "Oh my god. I feel so bad. If I'd known, of course I would've let you sleep! No wonder you were tired."

"Ah, sleep is overrated. And I couldn't let you go to the lake alone. It wasn't safe."

"But you didn't have to work at my clinic."

He shrugged. "Maybe not."

Detective DiNardo started to walk Nucci down the street, toward the police station. Tito followed along obediently. People had gathered on the street to watch the commotion, and so Nucci hung his head low. As DiNardo led Nucci past Audrey, Nucci came to a stop, and Audrey braced herself for the tirade. Maybe he'd even spit in her face.

Instead, he said, "Please. Take my Tito. He's a good boy. Find him a good home."

She reached down and took the dog by his collar. "Yes. Of course I will."

He nodded with gratitude before walking down the road, not stopping to look back at his poor pup, who started to whine.

It tugged at Audrey's heart. She reached down and stroked his brindle fur, patting his broad side heartily. "Aw, poor you. Don't worry. We will find you a good home." She stood up and murmured, "Even if it's with me."

Mason raised an eyebrow. "Why do you look terrified about that? Big dog like that'll probably keep you in line."

She shrugged. "It's just that you know how busy I am. This dog needs walks all the time, especially with someone who can keep up with him while he's running."

Mason nodded thoughtfully. "Well… what about me?"

She snorted. "Ha. Be serious."

"I *am* serious." He thrust up his chin. "I ain't always joking around."

Her jaw dropped. "I don't know. It's a big responsibility. He needs someone who's going to love him. Not call him an 'it' and get all grossed out whenever he drools on his precious things."

Mason crouched in front of the dog and ran a hand through his ears. "I actually had a dog like this when I was a kid. Named him Snoopy."

She blinked. "You did?"

"Yeah. Died when I was twelve. Worst day of my life."

She stared at him, shocked and a little touched by the show of emotion on his face. No wonder he'd been weird around Polpetto. Maybe it was more about hurt than disgust. She'd lost her first dog around the time she turned twelve, too, at about the same time her father disappeared. Those two things, happening so close together, were like the end of her world. "It's always hardest to lose your first best friend."

"Yeah." He grinned at the animal. "Maybe it's about time I get myself a second one. What do you say, Polpetto?"

In answer, he let out a sharp bark and handed Mason his paw. Mason laughed and shook it, and the deal was made.

CHAPTER TWENTY SEVEN

Later that day, Audrey made it a point to stop by the Regalpetra on *Via Garibaldi*. Cradling the bottle of wine under her arm, she walked into the simple but well-appointed hotel's lobby and went straight to the reception desk.

"Buongiorno," she said, trying to remember the basic Italian phrases she learned from that guidebook. *Um, how do you say, Can I have a person's room number?* "Uh, Bruno Altavera?"

The woman with a shiny black bob, in a blazer with a shiny brass placard that said, "Diana," typed something into a computer. "Ah," she said with a bright smile shining between her red-painted lips. "Our American friend, yes?"

Audrey nodded. "I am also an American friend," she admitted.

"Is Mr. Altavera expecting you?"

"No. Actually, I just wanted to give him this gift." She tittered. "You see, there was a little misunderstand—"

"I've found that Mr. Altavera is not very good with surprises," she said, eyeing the bottle in Audrey's hand. "It might be better that you just leave the bottle here, and I'll make sure he gets it."

Audrey's lips twisted to the side. "Well, I would. I wanted to tell him something, and apologize, too."

The woman pushed across a notepad with the hotel's ornate crest on the top. "You can write a note."

Audrey nodded and set the wine on the counter. "Okay."

She picked up the pen and wrote: *Dear Mr. Altavera.*

That was the easy part. She tapped her chin with the pen, trying to decide how to form her next words. *I'm sorry I nearly got you thrown in a Sicilian prison the second time I met you.* She winced. *I'm sorry you missed your flight home because of my rash suspicions.* She clenched her teeth harder. *I'm sorry you probably not only hate Sicily but all of Italy as well and will probably never even set foot in an American pizza place again, as long as you live.*

"Audrey?"

She whirled around, pen still in her hand, to see Bruno stepping off a gilded elevator, a questioning expression on his face.

"Oh, hi! I brought you—" She waved at it so frantically that she knocked the wine off the counter. It fell to the white marble floor and shattered across it, splattering red all over the place, especially on her khaki pants. On the white tile, it looked like something out of a crime scene.

Behind her, Diana said, "No problem. We'll have someone clean that."

Audrey sighed. There went thirty euros, right down the drain.

He approached, careful to avoid the minefield of broken glass. "What are you doing here?"

"I brought you a peace offering," she said. "At least, I tried to. Sorry."

He surveyed the broken pieces of glass between them. "Peace offering?"

"Oh. You probably haven't heard the news. They arrested Mimi Catalano's killer earlier this afternoon."

"They did? Huh." He stuck his lower lip out and nodded with satisfaction. "Pretty good. I thought I'd be stuck here for weeks. So who was it?"

"It was a man who'd lost his dog. It turned out Mimi Catalano was going around the lake properties, letting out dogs and trying to make them strays in order to pass this tax that she's been trying to promote."

"That so?" He stroked his fleshy chin, staring at hers. "Uh, you have something …"

"What?" She wiped her chin and inspected her fingers. They were covered in a smear of black ink. "Oops." She began to rub it harder, then lifted it for his inspection. "Did I get it?"

"Uh …" He said it in a way that made her think she wasn't even close. "Almost. Well, I always knew it wasn't me, and eventually they'd find that out."

"Anyway. I wanted to bring you something to say that I was sorry." Still rubbing her chin, she looked down at the floor, where a hotel worker was kneeling between them, trying to sweep up the mess with an inadequate hand broom and dustpan. "And… I fouled that up, too. But I promise to get you a new bottle before you leave."

"It's all right. And to tell you the truth, I don't think I'm leaving," he said, stepping out of the way of the worker as he tried to mop up some wine by his foot. "When I got back here, I called my girl, and she said that it was all right that I was being kept here. She'd heard everything I said about the place and wanted to come out herself. So she took some time off from work and she'd going to be on the next plane out here. So we'll stick around here together for a few more days, and make the decision together."

"Really?" She clapped her hands together in front of her. "That's wonderful."

"Yeah, and, to tell you the truth…" He leaned forward, as if he had a great secret to tell her. He reached into his pocket and pulled out a platinum diamond solitaire. "I have been holding onto this baby for months, but haven't been able to think of a way to pop it to her, if you know what I mean. What better way than in front of that castle, surrounded by the mountains?"

"Yes!" Audrey said, as if she were the bride, because for a moment she'd gotten transported by the idea of it. Who knew that rough-looking Bruno, who looked like one of those guys who enjoyed nothing more than a beer and football game on Sunday, was a romantic? "I agree. That would be perfect. Well, I will send you another bottle of wine to congratulate you."

"Yeah? That's a deal."

She smiled. "Good luck!" She looked down at the man cleaning the mess. "And I'll bring *you* a bottle, too, *signore*. I'm so sorry for the mess."

*

That evening, Audrey poured herself a glass of wine and started to tile the kitchen, which Mason, true to his word, had finished sanding that afternoon. As she was starting to place the first tile, a text came through from her sister: *So, question.*

That sounded like a lead-in to a long conversation. She stopped, peeled off her gloves, and responded with: *One sec. I'll call you*

Brina picked up the second she dialed the phone, almost before it rang. "Yes?"

"I'm just sitting here, thinking. He brought you dinner. He sanded the floor for you. He volunteered in your clinic. He adopted a pet for you. He's hotter than Hades. WOMAN. What is stopping you from jumping him right now?"

Back to jumping again. Audrey sighed, and her mouth watered a little at the thought of that hot brown. She'd told Brina everything that had happened in the last few days, hoping to get some of that stellar big-sister advice. But though Mason seemed to like her, she couldn't quite grasp the idea that he *liked her*, liked her. Yes, it was very middle school, but Audrey usually felt that way, where relationships were concerned. The man had clearly been around the block before, and she hadn't even left the front yard.

"What makes you think he isn't just being nice because I'm his only American friend in town?"

"Please. Nice would be saying 'Good morning' when he passes you on the street. This is BEYOND nice. Trust me."

"Come on. Don't give me that."

"I'm not giving you anything but the truth."

Maybe. Brina knew these things, especially when it came to men. But Mason? He was too good-looking. Too perfect. If he ever gazed meaningfully into her eyes, like he wanted to kiss her, she'd probably have a heart attack. Besides, that would never happen…

"But he has a guest coming soon. A woman. Probably a girlfriend. A beautiful, supermodel girlfriend with a name like Amanda. He's kind of quiet and mysterious about his past. I still think he's definitely just being nice."

"Ugh. Would you stop being like that?"

"Like what?"

"Like, selling yourself short. You're a doctor! And a darn fine-looking woman. You need to get more confidence, girl. Don't mind when I say I TOLD YOU SO when he professes his undying love."

Audrey snorted. If he did that, she'd *definitely* have a heart attack. "I don't have time to think about that. I have a pet adoption day to plan."

"What about your bio—"

"Stop it with the biological clock crap. I am just *fine*."

Brina let out a dramatic sigh. "Right. Planning your pet adoption extravaganza is so high on your list. I get it."

"Well, yes. It's important!"

The second she said it, she realized how lame she sounded. Brina laughed. "Okay, but when you're eighty and an old cat lady who talks to her animals like they're her best friends, don't say I didn't warn you."

She pressed her lips together. "I'll never do that." She looked over at Nick, who was busy preening his tail. "I don't talk to animals like they're my best friends, do I, Nick?"

Oh, God. "I've got to go."

She set the phone aside, placed and smoothed the mortar, and affixed the first row of tiles. Not bad, not bad. Thanks to Mason's sanding, the kitchen was going to be *fantastic* when it was done. She'd done this before, with her father, and of course, always had his expertise to rely on. Now, it was almost as if she could hear his voice, strong and gentle, guiding her. *Make sure it's level. Right. Just like that. Perfect.*

Before she knew it, a tear trickled down her cheek and landed on the mortar. She wiped it away, reached for her glass of wine, and took a big gulp. She didn't need to be getting sad now.

She cracked her knuckles and prepared to do another row when someone rapped on the door. Jumping over the tile cutter, she rushed to answer it.

Thank goodness, it was Orlando Falco. She'd been waiting impatiently to hear the results of the vote all day. Luckily, she'd had quite a few interesting activities to fill her time, but it'd been on her mind ever since he'd told her about it.

She wanted to ask him, but she also didn't want to be rude. "Hello, Signore Falco. Come on in. Can I get you some wine?"

He looked around the place. "Ah. Nice tile. So you're proceeding with the renovations on your lovely home, I see."

"Yep. Keeping busy." *Tell me what the outcome was. Please?* She held up the bottle to him. "Wine?"

He nodded. "That would be lovely."

She poured him a glass and handed it to him. "You've got me on the edge of my seat. Was there an outcome to the vote?"

He nodded and a small smile crept onto his face. "Denied."

"What?" She jumped so suddenly she sent wine from her own glass sloshing onto her hand. Shaking it off, she reached forward to him to toast. "I'd say this definitely calls for a celebration."

He clinked glasses with her. "I agree. *Salud.*" He took a sip. "The rumors have gotten out that Mimi Catalano was intentionally trying to flood the streets of Mussomeli with strays to further her case for the tax. And because of that, the council members agreed that perhaps it isn't as big a problem as she made it out to be. And so we all agreed to give the clinic time to work before we attempted other measures."

"Good choice." She sipped her wine. Finally free of the tax worries, all those grand ideas she'd had for the clinic competed for attention in her mind. She wasn't sure what to ask him about first. "I'm sure once the rumor gets out, I'll be getting a lot more calls from people missing their pets, if Mimi was indeed doing that. Maybe we can make a few matches."

"Yes. I hope."

"And I've been kind of planning it on the down low, but now I can really get things moving. I want to have a pet adoption day right away.

Maybe two Saturdays from now? We're already getting close to a full house. I'll waive the adoption fee for anyone who takes in one of our strays. What do you think?"

Falco smiled. "Yes, that would be wonderful. Let me know what I can do to help. Dottore Smart, I always knew you were the best one for this job."

EPILOGUE

On a bright Saturday afternoon, the clinic was packed with animals and people alike.

Audrey sat behind the reception desk and watched the Meet and Greet. So many people, interested in adopting one of the many strays that had made their way into the clinic. So many children, giggling with delight. So many smiles, contented purrs, and happy barks.

All in all, a very good day.

"I think you can call this a success," Orlando Falco said to her with a smile. "How many adoption applications have you gotten in?"

"Ten, so far," she said, counting the papers. "More to come, hopefully."

"That means ten new clients for you."

Yes, that was the point of waiving the fee. She'd collect a salary to keep this place running later, when they came in for their wellness visits and shots, and when they recommended their friends to her. But that was a small price to pay for all the love and happiness the animals would give them in return. There really was nothing more special than helping an animal find its fur-ever home.

As she was watching a little boy cuddling a giant white lop-eared bunny on his lap, petting it gently while the animal shivered in delight, someone approached and threw her big purse on the counter. "I'll take this one. How much?"

She looked up to see Nessa unzipping her wallet. "Which one?"

She sighed, bent down, and lifted a giant gray cat into her arms, holding it like it was a foreign object. "This one."

"Seriously?" When Nessa put it down and nodded impatiently, she said, "This isn't like checkout at the supermarket, Nessa. You have to fill out an application first."

Her eyebrows came together. "How long will that take?"

"I'm doing approvals on the spot, but—"

"Good. I need him because I think he'll add so much to my HGTV show. Filming is starting next week, you know. Imagine me, petting my cat on the sofa, while they're interviewing me. People love… animals. So they'll automatically love me." She wrinkled her nose. "Not that they wouldn't already, but …"

"Um," Audrey said, already knowing there was no way she'd let her pass muster, if that was her reasoning for owning a pet. Cue months, even years, of unneighborly interaction. "Nessa, a pet is not a prop. It's a lot of work. That's one of the first things we ask on the application—whether you're ready to assume that responsibility. And didn't you mention you were going to flip the house and leave soon?"

"Change in plans. My agent's thinking bigger. Season two. He's talking about me fixing up and flipping more houses in town. If I do that, I'll need a home base." She looked down at the animal. "And a cat."

Gnawing on her lip, Audrey grabbed the application and handed it to Nessa on a clipboard, already knowing this wouldn't end well. *Like the people who adopt bunnies just for Easter, anyone who needs a cat just for Hollywood is a disaster waiting to happen. Great. Nessa's going to hate me even more when she gets the ol' APPLICATION DENIED stamp.* "Just fill this out. The adoption fee is waived if you're accepted, today only."

Nessa threw her purse on her shoulder, tucked the clipboard under her arm, and picked up the cat. "Come on, Lambchop baby, let's go make this official," she said, stroking her fur gently.

Lambchop baby? Hmm. Audrey watched her carefully make her way to a seat and settle the cat comfortably down on her lap before beginning to fill out the form. The cat curled there, looking completely content, as Nessa put pen to paper, still stroking the cat's fur with her other hand.

Well… maybe… and hey. If Nessa loved something other than herself, maybe there was hope for her after all. Maybe she and Nessa could even be… gasp… *friends* one day.

"Hey."

Audrey swung her head back to the entrance at the sound of the familiar voice. It was Mason, standing with his new pet mastiff. She hadn't seen him in a while, since he'd taken some time from volunteering at the clinic to help his new pet get settled and was also busy getting his house fixed up for his guest. She jumped up and ran around the counter, petting the dog's fur. He had a brand new collar on. She lifted the charm on it and read, *Polpetto*.

"Oh! You changed his name?"

Mason shrugged. "No doubt about it. He's definitely a Polpetto."

"You haven't brought him in! I feel like I haven't seen you in ages. How are things going?"

"They're going," he said stiffly.

"Are you sure?" she asked him, worried. Yes, he'd had a dog before, but that was a long time ago. And there was nothing sadder than when pet and owner didn't make a good match. "Nothing bothering you about him? I can help. I know it can be an adjustment."

He scratched the back of his neck, something she'd already started to learn he only did when he was nervous about something. "Nope. Everything's good."

She couldn't figure out what might be wrong with him until she looked behind him and noticed an older woman with white blond hair cast up in perfect ringlets over her head, a fully made-up face, and a smart black suit with a rose-colored silk scarf around her neck. She looked like a wealthy society lady who'd gotten lost on her way to the tea shop.

Audrey straightened, and, because something about this woman's perfection made her feel even less so, smoothed down her hair. "Can I help—"

"Aren't you going to introduce me to your friend, Mason?" she cooed in a sweet southern accent, offering Audrey her pale hand. She had hand-model fingers, thin like flower stems, with a flawless manicure and a blindingly giant rock on her ring finger.

Audrey took the tips of her fingers and shook them gently. That was it, the woman was a Southern belle. She smelled like a rose garden. And she was Mason's...

Mason jumped between the two of them. "I was just gonna. Audrey's the veterinarian here. Audrey, this is Constance Rose Jackson-DeWitt." He was rubbing the back of his neck even harder now. "My momma."

Audrey's widened. "Oh! So you're visiting us from the States? Did you just come from Charleston, too?"

She nodded. "I did. Had to see how my baby boy was getting along. He's never been away from us. This is a big change for him."

Audrey glanced at Mason, who now had a pleasant, little-boy blush beneath his flawless tan. "Momma ..." he warned in a low voice.

"Mason's my littlest. And he's always had a little trouble leaving the nest. When he got this idea in his head, we all thought he was plum crazy. A house for a dollar. My husband, god rest his soul, was a businessman. He made his wealth on risk. But this? I told Mason that he'd be rolling over in his grave if he ever heard such a cockamamie scheme."

"Momma."

She grabbed onto his arm and shook it a little. "But here he is! And doin' a wonderful job with his place. So you got yourself one of these little shacks for a dollar, too? You're a plucky one. And a doctor?"

Audrey nodded. "Yes. This is my clinic. I only moved her a couple months ago, so it's not much, but it's getting there."

She clasped her hands together. "Oh, it's very nice. Very sweet. The whole town is. I was so worried about Macy gettin' on around here but I think I got nothin' to worry about."

Macy? Beside her, Mason was fidgeting like a kid made to stand in the corner at school. Audrey stifled the giggle threatening to explode from her lips and said, "Yes. It's very safe. Very nice. I really have had nothing but positive experiences."

"Though I have to say..." She leaned in a little. "How you got him to adopt this big dog is beyond me. He was broken apart when his Snoopy died. That was his baby. I thought he'd never love another."

She looked over at Mason. "He told me Polpetto has had his share of heartbreak, too. So I think they are going to be great for each other."

She smiled and fanned her face. "Well, butter my biscuit, I'm burning up. I gotta get outside and get me some air. It sure was nice meeting you. Putting a face with the name."

Audrey's heart skipped in her chest. So that meant Mason had told her mother about her? What a little mama's boy. Now, she really wanted to text Brina this major development. Brina would know exactly what this meant.

"Likewise," she said.

"You should come over to his place for dinner," she continued with a smile. "Maybe on Sunday? I'm gonna make my famous chicken and waffles. Macy's really missed that, poor kid. He's gettin' so skinny."

She squeezed his side and he jumped, flashing her an annoyed look. Then he nodded and scratched the back of his neck. "Yeah. You should come."

Audrey nodded, her heart thumping louder. "Uh. Okay. Sure. I like waffles."

"Perfect!" The woman flounced out on high heels of the same bright pink color as her scarf, leaving a cloud of rose perfume in her wake. One of the cats managed to invade it and ran away, hair standing on end, mewling like it'd walked through a cloud of Agent Orange.

Before he left, Mason leaned in. "Now you know why I didn't want to tell you about her."

So he *was* being deliberately vague. "Why? She's so sweet... *Macy!*"

He gave her a warning look. "Don't call me that. No one calls me that. That there's just the airs she puts on to impress people. She's so stuck up, she'd drown in a rainstorm."

"Hey. That isn't a nice thing to say about the woman who gave you life!"

"Yeah, and she reminds me every day how she can take it away from me." He gave her an apologetic look. "Anyway, you try livin' with her. All she's been doin' is complainin' since I picked her up at the airport yesterday. Car's too small, road's too narrow, bathroom don't have a freaking bidet."

Audrey laughed. "Wow. Well, it was really nice meeting your mysterious guest, finally."

He nodded, then looked like he was about to say something else. As he leaned in, G appeared in the door. *"Principessa!"*

Mason let out a groan as G approached. Mason tapped the counter and murmured, "See you later," then made a quick exit, glaring at G as he did.

Really… what was with that?

"Hi, G!" she said as he laid a tray in front of her. "Come to adopt a little pet for your place?"

He shook his head and pulled a checkered napkin off the tray to reveal some beautiful cannoli. "Not today. But I brought dessert for your friends."

She smiled. "Yum. You're so nice," she said, taking them from him.

"And… I wanted to see if you are busy, for your next day off?"

That was Sunday. "Actually, I am. But—"

He pouted. "I wanted to take you out to see the sights. Don't make me wait too long."

"I won't. Maybe next Sunday?"

"All right, it's a date."

She smiled and motioned around. "What do you think?"

He nodded with approval. "I think that Mussomeli is lucky to have you."

As she looked around at the clinic, at the smiling faces, at everything she had accomplished so far, all because she'd decided to take a dollar chance…she could hardly believe it.

For once in her life, it seemed as if fate was smiling her way.

NOW AVAILABLE!

A VILLA IN SICILY: VINO AND DEATH
(A Cats and Dogs Cozy Mystery—Book 3)

"Very entertaining. Highly recommended for the permanent library of any reader who appreciates a well-written mystery with twists and an intelligent plot. You will not be disappointed. Excellent way to spend a cold weekend!"
--Books and Movie Reviews (regarding *Murder in the Manor*)

A VILLA IN SICILY: VINO AND DEATH is book #3 in a charming new cozy mystery series by bestselling author Fiona Grace, author of *Murder in the Manor*, a #1 Bestseller with over 100 five-star reviews (and a free download)!

Audrey Smart, 34, has made a major life change, walking away from her life as a vet (and from a string of failed romance) and moving to Sicily to buy a $1 home—and embark on a mandatory renovation she knows nothing about.

Audrey is busy working to open the town's new shelter, while also renovating her own problematic home—and dating again. With the help of friends, she begins taking in sick strays. But not everyone in town is grateful for her services, and she soon makes unexpected enemies.

Audrey's small Sicilian town hires a new building inspector to deal with the influx of $1 home owners—and he sets about making Audrey's idyllic Sicilian life utterly miserable. Just when things can't get any worse, the inspector turns up dead—leaving Audrey as the main suspect.

Audrey, without an alibi, is under more pressure than she's ever been to solve the crime. But the inspectors list of enemies was long.

Very, very long.

Can she solve this impossible case?

A laugh-out-loud cozy packed with mystery, intrigue, renovation, animals, food, wine—and of course, love—A VILLA IN SICILY will capture your heart and keep you glued to the very last page.

"The book had heart and the entire story worked together seamlessly that didn't sacrifice either intrigue or personality. I loved the characters - so many great characters! I can't wait to read whatever Fiona Grace writes next!"
--Amazon reviewer (regarding *Murder in the Manor*)

"Wow, this book takes off & never stops! I couldn't put it down! Highly recommended for those who love a great mystery with twists, turns, romance, and a long lost family member! I am reading the next book right now!"
--Amazon reviewer (regarding *Murder in the Manor*)

"This book is rather fast paced. It has the right blend of characters, place, and emotions. It was hard to put down and I hope to read the next book in the series."
--Amazon reviewer (regarding *Murder in the Manor*)

Fiona Grace

Fiona Grace is author of the LACEY DOYLE COZY MYSTERY series, comprising nine books (and counting); of the TUSCAN VINEYARD COZY MYSTERY series, comprising six books (and counting); of the DUBIOUS WITCH COZY MYSTERY series, comprising three books (and counting); of the BEACHFRONT BAKERY COZY MYSTERY series, comprising six books (and counting); and of the CATS AND DOGS COZY MYSTERY series, comprising six books.

Fiona would love to hear from you, so please visit www.fionagraceauthor.com to receive free ebooks, hear the latest news, and stay in touch.

BOOKS BY FIONA GRACE

LACEY DOYLE COZY MYSTERY
MURDER IN THE MANOR (Book#1)
DEATH AND A DOG (Book #2)
CRIME IN THE CAFE (Book #3)
VEXED ON A VISIT (Book #4)
KILLED WITH A KISS (Book #5)
PERISHED BY A PAINTING (Book #6)
SILENCED BY A SPELL (Book #7)
FRAMED BY A FORGERY (Book #8)
CATASTROPHE IN A CLOISTER (Book #9)

TUSCAN VINEYARD COZY MYSTERY
AGED FOR MURDER (Book #1)
AGED FOR DEATH (Book #2)
AGED FOR MAYHEM (Book #3)
AGED FOR SEDUCTION (Book #4)
AGED FOR VENGEANCE (Book #5)
AGED FOR ACRIMONY (Book #6)

DUBIOUS WITCH COZY MYSTERY
SKEPTIC IN SALEM: AN EPISODE OF MURDER (Book #1)
SKEPTIC IN SALEM: AN EPISODE OF CRIME (Book #2)
SKEPTIC IN SALEM: AN EPISODE OF DEATH (Book #3)

BEACHFRONT BAKERY COZY MYSTERY
BEACHFRONT BAKERY: A KILLER CUPCAKE (Book #1)
BEACHFRONT BAKERY: A MURDEROUS MACARON (Book #2)
BEACHFRONT BAKERY: A PERILOUS CAKE POP (Book #3)
BEACHFRONT BAKERY: A DEADLY DANISH (Book #4)
BEACHFRONT BAKERY: A TREACHEROUS TART (Book #5)
BEACHFRONT BAKERY: A CALAMITOUS COOKIE (Book #6)

CATS AND DOGS COZY MYSTERY
A VILLA IN SICILY: OLIVE OIL AND MURDER (Book #1)
A VILLA IN SICILY: FIGS AND A CADAVER (Book #2)
A VILLA IN SICILY: VINO AND DEATH (Book #3)
A VILLA IN SICILY: CAPERS AND CALAMITY (Book #4)

A VILLA IN SICILY: ORANGE GROVES AND VENGEANCE
(Book #5)
A VILLA IN SICILY: CANNOLI AND A CASUALTY (Book #6)